"Goodness Agnes!" Elliot exclaimed. His satchel slid from his shoulder but he didn't seem to notice. Instead, it dragged behind him and nearly caught in his kite-string lifeline. The torchlight exposed the messy condition of the room. Artifacts were stacked one upon another, some lay strewn near a wall, others lay on the mudbrick as if dropped in a hurry.

"This . . ." Elliot's words squeezed into a hush. A sudden brightness seemed to surround them, as if someone had opened the curtains in a dark room. Silently, he motioned them into the treasure room. As they entered, their torchlight entered with them—but the orange glow remained in the catacombs.

"Torches," Kasha said quietly.

Elliot's face tensed.

"We've got company."

Join Rachel and Elliot on all
their adventures!

TRUTHQUEST

The Mountain That Burns Within
Valley of the Giant
Treasure of the Hidden Tomb

Treasure of the Hidden Tomb

Tad Hardy

ChariotVICTOR
PUBLISHING
A DIVISION OF COOK COMMUNICATIONS

Chariot Books is an imprint of ChariotVictor Publishing
Cook Communications, Colorado Springs, CO 80918
Cook Communications, Paris, Ontario
Kingsway Communications, Eastbourne, England

TREASURE OF THE HIDDEN TOMB
© 1997 by Tad Hardy

ISBN 0-78143-003-8
Edited by Mandy Finkler
Designed by Andrea Boven
Cover illustration by John Lytle
Map illustration by Guy Wolek
First printing, 1997
Printed in the United States of America
01 00 99 98 97   5 4 3 2 1

For Mari

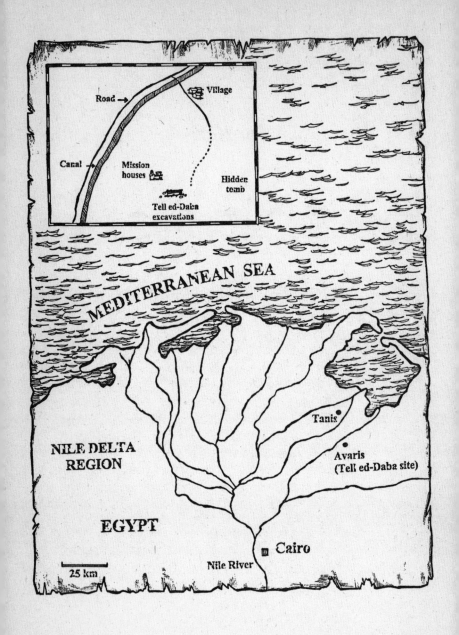

Road →

Village

Canal →

Mission houses

Hidden tomb

Tell ed-Daba excavations

MEDITERRANEAN SEA

NILE DELTA REGION

Tanis

Avaris (Tell ed-Daba site)

EGYPT

Cairo

Nile River

25 km

Places and Things in Egypt

Cairo (KIE-row) the capital of Egypt; a very large, modern city

Canopic jars (kuh-NOE-pik JAR-s) ancient Egyptian jars or vases used to hold the remains of the dead

catacombs (KAT-uh-KOMES) underground chambers or tunnels with areas for graves

hieroglyph (HIGH-ruh-GLIFF) ancient Egyptian writing method using pictures to represent words or sounds

obelisk (AH-buh-lisk) a tall, four-sided stone pillar that comes to a pyramid-shaped point

Qintar (KIN-tar) a city in northeastern Egypt

sarcophagus (sar-KOFF-uh-gus) a stone or wooden coffin, used for mummies in ancient Egypt

scarab (SCARE-ub) a type of beetle, or sculpture of this beetle

Tell ed-Daba (TELL ed-DAH-bah) an archeological site in Egypt's northeastern Nile Delta

CHAPTER 1

"Okay, here's another one," Rachel read aloud. "What do mummies drink for breakfast?"

"Orange juice," Elliot replied. He was not paying attention, focusing instead on the odd-shaped stone in front of him at the small table.

"Oh, you're not even trying!" she snapped back. "They drink powdered milk! Get it? *Powdered*? As in mummy dust?" She turned the page in her riddle book. "Now . . . what kind of music do mummies like to dance to?" No reply.

"*Wrap* music!" She couldn't contain her laughter.

"Sorry, Rachel, what was the question?"

"How do you expect to get these riddles when you're not even listening?" she huffed. "Here, try this one. How many mummies does it take to screw in a light bulb?"

"Uhh . . . one, I guess." Elliot pulled the table lamp closer and held the stone artifact beneath it for a better look.

"None, silly. Mummies don't need light bulbs!" She

let out a cackle, which finally captured her cousin's attention. He wrinkled his brow in response.

"That's not even funny."

"Of course it is! I made that one up myself."

Elliot set the artifact aside and, with a heavy sigh, rested his chin in his hands below his wire-rimmed glasses.

"Now," Rachel continued, "what do you call a mummy footrace across the desert?" She stifled a giggle as she read the solution to herself. Then she called out the answer. "A dead heat! Get it? A dead heat!"

"Yes, Rachel, I get it."

"See if you can get this one, Archeology King . . . What sort of flowers do mummies grow?"

"Dried flowers." At least he was trying to muster an answer now.

"No. Chrysantha-mummies." She laughed loudly again.

"I'm surprised the Egyptian customs officer didn't confiscate that book at the airport."

"*He* had a sense of humor." She closed the book then let it fall open to a new page. Elliot quickly reached across the small table and closed it back up.

"You're no fun," she announced. She slipped the book into her waist pack that was slung across the hotel bedpost. "So . . . when do we go dig up mummies?"

"Uh . . . Rachel . . . "

"I read all of those books, you know," she went on. "*Curse of the Mummy's Pyramid, My Uncle Was an Alien Mummy, The Mummy Ate My Homework.* I've even learned a saying in ancient mummy language that keeps mummies away from a person's tea. You say . . . "

"Rachel?"

"What?"

"We won't be digging up any mummies." Elliot sounded quite certain.

"We won't?" Her shoulders slumped. "Then why have we come to Egypt? Isn't that why people come to Egypt?"

"Not exactly." Elliot paused to blow across the surface of the etched stone block before him, then returned to brushing it with a hand-held whisk broom. With each swipe of the broom, the faint outline of a fat hippopotamus grew clearer. "Dad's here for the archeological conference, remember?"

"As are all of those other dirt-diggers here in the hotel," Rachel added. She pulled up a chair and sat next to her cousin and his stone hippo. "Which of them gave you this ugly thing?"

"Dr. Eppling, from the Rockefeller Museum. He bought it from a peddler yesterday at some open market south of Cairo." He squinted at the rock block. "Y'know, it's amazing . . . here we are surrounded by modern cities with millions of people, yet almost anyone can scavenge ancient artifacts like this every day, out in the desert. Most aren't worth much—the artifacts, that is—in fact, some of them are fakes. But the real ones like this hippo are a true part of Egyptian history. I'm just glad Dr. Eppling spotted it."

"You sound like some blasted telly commercial for archeology!" Rachel said, pleased to hear her own

British accent have the last word with her brainy
cousin. She pulled Elliot's dirty dig-site hat, the one
Elliot wore everywhere except in the shower, from his
head and pressed it down on her own. "And now . . . a
word from our sponsor," she said grandly, staring at
Elliot as if he were a television camera. "We are the
archeologists, although intelligent people—such as
Ms. Rachel Ashton—call us dirt-diggers. We're a boring lot, we are—we've gotten that way from spending
our days talking to rocks. But without us you might
never have known that people carved stone hippopotami
and buried them ten million years ago."

"More like four thousand years ago," Elliot butted in.

"Whatever." She looked down her nose at him and
continued her commentary. "We make trips around the
world and find bits of clay pots, then place them in
museums so you can pay hundreds of dollars to see
them. Our mission is to save the past for your future!"
She pointed directly at Elliot with a dramatic snap of
her wrist.

Elliot adjusted the wire-rimmed glasses sitting on his
nose. A smile slowly spread over his face.

"Not bad, Rachel. I kind of liked that—the last bit, I
mean, about saving the past for our future. Maybe you
can perform at the conference later." He snatched
back his hat before she could stop him.

"Conference indeed." Rachel scooted her chair away
from the small table where Elliot's makeshift hippo lab
lay scattered about. "This is the third day of the Coyote
Conference— "

"Cairo," he corrected her.

"Whatever, and I'm quite tired of it if you must know," she huffed. "You and Uncle Mason trot off to meetings while I'm left to explore all of the exciting places Uncle Mason allows me to visit—the lobby, the breakfast bar, the hotel exercise room. I didn't travel all day and all night, from Kentucky to here, just to watch sweaty people sit in hot tubs."

"Maybe if you hadn't gotten into that argument with the fruit peddler the first day, Dad would let you explore a little farther."

"That peddler," Rachel began, her temper rising, "was a complete dolt. He was rude and snappy. Besides, I never intended to upset his entire fruit cart. He wouldn't even speak to me in English!"

"Goodness Agnes, Rachel!" Elliot exclaimed. "He's Egyptian—he probably doesn't speak English!"

"Oh, you're just standing up for him. I imagine he gave you a free piece of fruit, Mr. Junior Archeology Pants." She waited for his reply.

"Only after I helped straighten his cart. Look, there's a short conference meeting on obelisks this afternoon before the field trip to the Egyptian Museum. Why don't you come along?"

"No, thank you. I needn't learn any more about wobble disks than I know already. I would rather be bored alone than be bored with two hundred crusty dirt-diggers." She considered the prospect of yet another afternoon at the exercise room. "Are you absolutely certain there isn't a 'Dig-a-Mummy Day' scheduled before these dreadful meetings end?"

"Positive. We *are* going to a dig site up near Qintar

for a couple of days before we go home, though. Dad knows one of the archeologists there."

"Why wasn't I informed of this?" She asked suspiciously.

"I just found out his morning. Relax, okay? You've got to be flexible if you ever want to be a good archeologist."

"The only thing I want is to return to Kentucky, so I won't see you for the rest of the summer."

"That's what I like about you, Rachel. You always have such kind things to say. I'm not sure which I like best, your kindness or your wonderful attitude." He grinned his champion Elliot-grin that told her he had won again. Arguing with him was like herding cats. Impossible. Almost nothing frazzled this nearly-thirteen-year-old cousin of hers. She counted herself fortunate to live several hours away from Elliot and Uncle Mason. If she lived nearby, she and Elliot probably would be in school together, both in sixth grade, and she would have to put up with him *all* of the time.

"If you had to spend vacations with yourself, you would—" She stopped short.

"I *do* spend vacations with myself. Don't you?" Elliot's raised eyebrows told her she had already lost the battle.

"Oh, cork it. I don't know why Mother sends me on these ridiculous jaunts of yours—roaming hillsides, scratching bits of rust from crusty hunks of old dry metal, watching large people crawl in and out of hot tubs. On second thought, I *do* know why—it's because she's too busy running off to who-knows-where, so she sends *me* off to some other who-knows-where!"

"Cairo. Cairo, Egypt." Elliot was lacing his shoes.

"I know that! I saw the giant pyramids and the towers and the millions of buildings in the middle of the desert when we flew in here. And I saw the sign at the airport, too."

Suddenly Uncle Mason's wide shoulders leaned in through the hotel room doorway. With his khaki clothing and smooth gray beard, he looked exactly like an archeologist should look. In fact, he looked like most of the other conference-goers, who also happened to look exactly like archeologists. Except Uncle Mason was bigger and happier—sort of a gentle, polar bear archeologist.

"Obelisk conference in forty-five minutes," he called, his full, low voice sounding like that of a radio announcer. "Any takers?"

"I'll be ready, Dad." Elliot laid his hippopotamus to one side.

"Rachel?"

"No, thank you. I haven't much interest in gobble disks and all of that computer bother."

"You're sure?" Uncle Mason went on, chuckling. "They're serving lunch first. With tea."

"Tea?" she piped up. "Tea, really?" She rubbed her legs for a moment, then grabbed her shoes. "Well, I suppose I could come along . . . to help Elliot out with the parts he doesn't understand."

"I should warn you," her uncle cautioned. "If you eat lunch, you will be expected to attend the museum tour this afternoon. They have some astounding artifacts. I really believe you would enjoy the trip. We'll be boarding the buses for the museum tour around one o'clock. Who knows? Elliot might need someone to explain the museum pieces as well." Uncle Mason winked in her direction.

"Right. I'd best attend the tour . . . for Elliot's sake." She flipped her hair from her shoulder and looked sideways at Elliot. "Now, don't you worry. I'll be happy to answer any questions you have about the seminar, the tour, even about this magnificent city of Coyote."

Elliot and Uncle Mason corrected her in unison. "Cairo."

"Yes, quite. Just keeping you on your toes. Now, point me to the tea."

CHAPTER 2

The after-lunch bus ride through the streets of Cairo
was a lesson in survival. Rachel hoped they would
reach the museum in one piece, which they did—but
not before their driver nearly ran over a taxicab fighting for a parking spot. The bus won, giving them curb-
side delivery near the museum's front entrance. She
and Elliot were the first people off the bus. They waited near the museum doors as all three busloads of conference participants unloaded into the early summer
heat, dragging their cameras and jabbering about this-
Dynasty and that-Dynasty.

"So," Elliot said with a casual smile, "other than the
question and answer period, did you enjoy the obelisk
seminar?"

"I enjoyed the tea at lunch a great deal more." Her
jaws tightened in anger at the memory of the seminar.
Finally she threw up her hands. "How was I to know
that obelisks are tall stone towers?"

"You could have asked."

"I *did* ask! I asked the speaker when he finished his

talk. Didn't you hear me?"

"Uh-huh. So did three hundred other archeologists."

"Three hundred rude archeologists," she countered back. "You didn't hear me laughing at *their* questions, did you?"

"Asking questions is the only way to learn. But I think your question about whether gobble disks taste better boiled or fried sort of stumped him. And next time you might try sitting rather than standing on your chair."

"Oh, you're all such a formal lot, you dirt-diggers. I think your brains are mummified."

"Speaking of mummies . . . I told you about the mummy room here at the museum, right?"

"If talking about it day and night counts—yes, you most certainly did." She watched the last of the scientists depart the bus and fall in line behind them to enter the museum's large double doors. Elliot studied the multi-story building for a minute.

"It's different than I remembered," he said, his brow furrowing a bit.

"Pinker?" Rachel asked, laughing at the building's gaudy color scheme.

"It is sort of pink, isn't it?"

Elliot straightened his hat and stood on his tiptoes for a better look through the tall framed windows lining the front of the museum. A weighty pair of lion's-head door knockers hung from the door. Surrounding each knocker were gold-colored spikes poking from the door. The man in charge of the spiked doors politely greeted everyone entering, but Rachel could tell he was really a security guard. He wore a navy and white uniform, a black-billed cap, and had a large leashed dog that sat attentively at his side.

Once inside, Elliot immediately broke away from the group toward a set of rooms just off the main entrance area. Rachel chose a winding route of her own among the displays. Uncle Mason was right. The artifact collection was extraordinary. Stone statues, sculptures, paintings, exquisite jewelry—all were displayed in an airy openness of museum space that was several stories high. This was the Egypt she had expected. Closing the museum door on Cairo's hustle-bustle city life was like closing a door on 3,000 years of time. Egypt had indeed been a great civilization. Elliot had explained it all to her, of course—on the plane, at the hotel, in the evenings after those dry seminars. He and Uncle Mason blabbed with other archeologists about rocks and pots and shiny bangles. But seeing the magnificent works of these ancient people firsthand somehow made it all come alive. Hopefully nothing in Elliot's mummy room would come alive.

A quick search told her that Elliot had disappeared into some other museum area, probably making notes in that blasted diary of his he called a journal. She wandered away from the crowd of dirt-diggers headed for the Rosetta stone, climbed the stairs to the second floor, and, quite by accident, stumbled into The Room. This had to be the mummy room Elliot spoke of so often.

It was a large, spacious room filled with little more than emptiness, silence . . . and death. An armada of glass cases, each large enough to hold a body, floated in the dim light above the hard museum floor. Walkways for the living were created by open paths winding around the glass boxes. Each box lay a little below eye level—for Rachel, at least—creating an eerie sense of swimming through a sea filled with bobbing mummies. She shuddered as a tingle shot through her spine. Suddenly the mummy jokes and riddles she peppered Elliot with seemed childish compared to the real thing. A part of her wished she had never agreed to come to the museum in the first place. But another part, a bigger part, was fascinated with the idea of staring at a roomful of dead kings.

Carefully she approached one of the display cases. When she drew close, the clear form of a partially clothed mummy lay before her. Its head and neck lay exposed above the linen wrappings, casting a fuzzy-gray shadow on the floor of the case where it rested. Rachel leaned closer and her own faint shadow fell upon the ancient man in the box. His left arm was drawn across his chest, his hand clasped in a half fist. His bones were still covered with dark, bumpy scales of skin. Except for his ear, which stood curled and wrinkled like an orange peel that had been in the sun too long, and an odd bend in his nose, he looked very much like he had looked over 3,000 years ago when he held the title of Pharaoh. He didn't seem real . . . yet there he lay, his leathery mouth curled into a calm and peaceful pose.

"Goodness Agnes!" Elliot's hushed cry trailed away behind her as his footsteps entered the room. Rachel turned to face him, and their eyes met.

"Or maybe I should say 'Goodness Amenhotep.' Can you believe we're here? We're actually here!" Elliot removed his hat, a sure signal that he was deeply moved by the experience. Then, slowly, he made his way down an open aisle between the display cases, gawking at each mummy as he shuffled along. Rachel watched him for a moment or two, then her patience ran out.

"Oh, stop gaping at these wretched things! And you needn't whisper, by the way—they are dead . . . D-E-A-D. You won't wake them!"

He cracked a smile.

"I've waited years to come back here. Five years, in fact. The last time I was here was a family vacation with Dad . . . and Mom." His smile faded a bit. "I remember Mom really liked this place. You know that little crystal pyramid in my room back home? She got that for me, here in the museum gift shop."

Rachel knew by Elliot's expression that he had mixed feelings about the museum. The one common bond she and Elliot shared was family . . . or lack of it. Uncle Mason was family, of course, since he was both her uncle and Elliot's dad. But they also shared the absence of a mother. A real absence, in Elliot's case, and a scheduled absence in the case of her own mother. Sometimes she wondered which was worse.

"But of course," she answered, trying to lighten the conversation. "Isn't this just the ideal spot for a family vacation—an above-ground cemetery? I've already decided, this is the first place I intend to bring my husband and family. Let's see . . . first we tour the big cemetery near Lexington, next we swing by those pet burial plots in California, then we make a beeline straight here for a relaxing, three-day gawk at these leather-covered bones. Lovely time."

Elliot's smile returned.

"You'll probably marry an archeologist and spend your honeymoon here, breaking ground on some new dig site."

"I think not, Mummy-dust Brain."

A small tourist group, made up of a dozen elderly women and a museum tour guide, began filing into the room. The guide directed them to a set of displays at the far side of the open room and began rattling off unfamiliar names and dates, all of which ended in B.C. Rachel studied the group as Elliot slowly moved around the room, stopping to read the information plaques scattered among the mummy cases.

"Look at this!" he nearly burst out. "The mummy of Merenptah! According to one ancient timetable, he could be the Pharaoh of the Exodus!" He didn't bother reading the paragraph of information posted beside the display case. Obviously, he didn't need to. For all Rachel knew, he had written the information himself.

"Although," he continued, "some scholars have challenged that idea. Now they think the Exodus may have happened later—maybe a couple hundred years later."

"Amazing." Rachel feigned a yawn and patted her palm to her mouth loudly, making certain Elliot noticed her boredom. "If you ask me, *all* of these gentlemen should have been at the Exercise . . . maybe they wouldn't be so scrawny then. See that one there?" She pointed to a nearby mummy case where yet another ancient Pharaoh rested. "He looks like he has a chicken's neck!"

"It's not Exercise, it's Exodus—the time in history when the Hebrew slaves fled Egypt and followed Moses into the desert." Elliot looked at the mummy before them. "And you're right. They all have chicken necks. That's part of the mummification process. First they take the body—"

"Stop!" Rachel held up both hands. "Stop right there. I will not listen to your awful story about putting Pharaohs' stomachs in clay pots and replacing their eyeballs with rocks. It's disgusting."

"Disgusting but true," he replied, examining yet another mummy with his green-eyed curiosity. "The Egyptians had a lot of customs and rituals surrounding death and the afterlife. The process of carving out a dead Pharaoh's lungs and liver and storing them away in Canopic jars was one of them."

"If you bring that up again I'll see that *your* liver gets gathered into a Karaoke jar!"

Elliot just smiled.

"You think *that's* disgusting . . . you should hear what modern-day tomb robbers do with extra mummies."

Rachel, without realizing it, had backed herself into one corner of the mummy room as Elliot rattled on. There she discovered two glass cases tucked against the wall. Both had sheets of paper sealed in plastic folders taped to the cases instead of a formal information plaque. Both held mummies, displayed on their backs with arms folded across their chests. Based on her experience at SIMA, the Southern Indiana Museum of Archeology which Uncle Mason directed back in Indiana, she could tell these mummies were new acquisitions. Her eyes scanned one of the makeshift information sheets.

New Acquisition. ANONYMOUS female mummy recovered adjacent to ruins near Tell ed-Daba in the eastern Nile Delta region.

By now Elliot had worked his way over to a set of displays near where she stood. This was her opportunity to stump Mr. Know-It-All-And-Then-Some.

"All right, King of the Nile," she baited him, "I have a brain teaser for you."

He glanced up momentarily.

"Not another mummy riddle, I hope."

"Oh, no no no," she continued. "The 500 dollar question is . . . 'Who was . . . King Annie-Moses?'" A satisfied expression settled on her face. At the same time, she gloated over the confused look on her cousin's face.

"Annie-Moses?" he repeated. He thought for several long moments. "No such animal. You must be talking about King Amenhotep. There were three of them, by the way."

"Ohhhh, I'm so sorry. Shall we go for two out of three, then?"

Elliot stepped around several mummy cases on his way to her side, still wearing a puzzled look.

"No, really. There was no King Annie-Moses. I would have remembered him."

"You couldn't have remembered him. Because 'him'

is a 'her.' He is a she. It's *Queen* Annie-Moses. I believe
you need to 'bone up' on your Egyptian history, Mr.
Mummy Master. No pun intended, of course."

Elliot crossed his arms and adjusted his wire-rimmed
glasses.

"That wasn't a fair question . . ."

"On the contrary," Rachel butted in. "I believe it was
an absolutely marvelous question."

A narrow squint appeared behind his framed lenses.
Then a broad set of teeth showed in a smile.

"Come to think of it, there was no Queen Annie-
Moses either. Where did you get all this stuff?" He
walked past her to the mummy case.

"See?" she challenged.

"Goodness Agnes, Rachel! It says 'Anonymous'
mummy, not Annie-Moses. You know—anonymous—
as in don't know who it is."

"Yes, yes, I know that!" she lied. "I just wanted to see
how well you knew your female Pharaohs."

"Actually, there were a few female rulers. But I don't
think this is one of them." Elliot examined the unwrapped head, arms, and feet of the ancient woman in the
glass container. He leaned closer to the mummy and
quickly began to read the information sheet. "This
mummy is new! Well, not really new . . . it's over 3,000
years old. But it's new to the museum. They're still
staging it for display."

"Delta Airlines found it," Rachel informed him.

He shook his head slowly.

"Not quite. It was found in the Nile River Delta at . . .
hey!" He suddenly grasped her shoulders in excite-

ment. "This mummy came from the dig site we're headed for tomorrow! Tell ed-Daba! This is great. You may just get your 'Dig-a-Mummy Day' yet! Wait till I tell Dad!"

"You may let go of my shoulders now," she answered in a firm whisper. "And you can jolly well turn down your volume! Half the museum can hear you."

"Oh, sorry. Guess I got a little carried away."

The visitors across the room had stopped their guided tour to stare at the two cousins huddled in the corner. Rachel carefully shoved Elliot aside and, in her most formal British accent, addressed the group.

"Please pay him no mind. He believes he has stumbled onto a long-lost ancestor. Carry on." She then turned her attention back to Elliot. "Why must you embarrass me everywhere we go?" she whispered coarsely. With a final, mature wave to the tourists, she turned on her heels like a fashion model and bumped squarely into the mummy case. It jiggled dangerously for a moment and Rachel watched helplessly as the framed glass shifted from the impact. She cringed, closed her eyes, and waited for the tumbling mummy box to shatter into a million pieces.

CHAPTER 3

Instead of hearing the crash of breaking glass, Rachel heard only a *clink-clink*. She opened her eyes to see Elliot straining under the weight of the display case. His voice was half whisper, half grunt.

"Shove that support leg back under this corner for me, would you please?"

She did as he asked, sulking the whole time.

"It wouldn't have fallen," she finally announced as she watched him position the case safely back in place. He said nothing, but waved at the tour group which had watched the entire event.

"Maybe we should go see the stone sculptures," he whispered to her. "They're a little harder to knock over."

"Was that supposed to be funny?" she snapped. "It wasn't. You could have dropped that glass box on my foot, possibly severing my ankle. Then what would I do? I'd spend my remaining days on one foot, explaining to everyone how I was attacked by a mummy!"

As she lifted her foot to demonstrate, she stumbled

over something on the museum floor. Elliot caught her
before she fell. The same *clink-clink* sound she had
heard moments earlier again echoed around the room.

"Well . . . what have we here?" Elliot wondered aloud.
He knelt next to her.

"I haven't the foggiest," she shot back. "But whatever
it is, I'll see to it that the museum sweeper is fired for
leaving it lying around!"

"Hmmm." He put on his hat and retrieved a shiny
object lying at her feet. Then, to Rachel's dismay, he
sprawled flat on the floor and crawled beneath the
unstable mummy case.

"What . . . what are you doing?" she whispered
through clenched teeth. "Get up! Get up this instant,
before they send in that enormous dog from the
lobby!"

Elliot's head and shoulders were no longer visible.
Only his wiggling legs poked from under the case.
Finally she hissed loudly and kicked at his feet. He
emerged like an auto mechanic scooting from beneath
the frame of an ailing pickup truck. A shiny golden
object was pinched between his fingers.

"Looks like it fell through a crack on the underside of
this display case," he told her, rising to dust himself
off. "It also looks strangely familiar. I should know
what this is." As usual, Elliot seemed disappointed in
himself for not instantly recognizing the object. His
face held the same defeated look as when he lost a
game of video checkers to his computer—a rare event.

The doodad in his hand resembled a half moon made
of pure gold. It was nearly as long as his middle finger

and seemed tarnished, unlike all of the other gold artifacts on display.

"Is it jewelry of some sort?"

"Maybe," he mumbled. "More than likely it was a
burial good folded into the wrappings around this
mummy. I doubt the museum curators knew it was
there."

"Why don't you keep it? Sew it onto that dismal hat
of yours. . . . "

Elliot's eyes bugged out at her.

"Keep it? What do I look like . . . a tomb robber?"

Rachel pointed to the tanned remains in the box
beside them. "Well, what's she going to do with old
jewelry? Wear it to her next pyramid party? I say take
it back to the States and make it into something useful.
Like a necklace for me."

One eye cocked in her direction above his frown.

"I'll find a museum attendant and turn it in."

"Oh, you're such a prude sometimes. Just stuff it in
your vest and be done with it. The museum people
don't even know its here. You said so yourself."

"I do want to make an imprint of this thing before I
return it," he went on, ignoring her. "One way or
another I'll figure out what it is." He pulled a pencil and
paper from his leather-bound journal, placed the gold
artifact carefully against the second mummy case lid,
and pressed the paper over it. With smooth, even
strokes he rubbed the pencil lead across the paper surface. A detailed image materialized. Finely etched
Egyptian shapes emerged on the paper. "Hieroglyphs,"
he muttered to himself.

"Hiram who?" When he didn't answer, Rachel sighed loudly and again turned her attention to the female mummy. "What say we ask the old girl if we can keep the gold moon, shall we?" She rapped gingerly on the display case lid. "Pardon me, mum. I do hate to wake you, but I was wondering . . . my cousin here stumbled onto a faded bit of gold that seems to have fallen from your wrappings. Would you mind ever so much if he keeps it to dress up his grimy dig hat? You wouldn't? Oh, how kind of you." She leaned close to the glass lid. "Thank you. Thank—" A gasp caught in her throat.

Elliot was stuffing the paper imprint into his pocket. "What's the matter?"

"How terrible! How horribly awful!"

"What's wrong?" He rushed to her side, arms outstretched as if he expected the case to topple again.

"This mummy . . . it . . . I mean, she . . . she's missing a thumb!"

"No kidding?" Elliot adjusted his glasses and scrunched his face nearly flat against the lid of the case. After a long, studious look, he raised his head and shrugged his shoulders. "Right thumb, to be exact. Looks to me like it's completely gone."

Rachel stomped her foot. "Is that pea-brain of yours set on Vacuum Cycle? I just told you that!"

"And I just confirmed it. That makes two matching scientific opinions. I'd say there is no doubt . . . this mummy's thumb is definitely missing."

She considered choking him on the spot for being so contrary, but thought better of it. There were no empty glass boxes around in which to stuff him. Elliot plucked a small magnifying glass from his vest pocket. Pressing it next to his eyeglass lens, he took another peek at the thumbless mummy.

"Hmmmm." More peeking, more squinting. "Hmm-mmmm."

Finally he looked up and lowered the magnifying glass. "You know what I would name this mummy's tomb? 'Robbed.'"

"Rob? Rob who? I thought this was a female mummy."

"Robbed," he repeated. "Stripped, snitched, ransacked. By thieves."

"You mean burgled? Really? What makes you so certain her tomb was burgled?"

"Well, for one thing, her thumb." A second look through the magnifying glass brought his explanation. "It appears she had two thumbs when she died. From the way the tissue is torn, I'd say the missing thumb was lost recently. Museum personnel would have saved it or stuck it back on. Tomb robbers usually aren't so careful."

"Let me make certain I understand you correctly," Rachel said slowly. She traced her finger along the edge of the glass case as her mind entertained a most wonderful idea. "We're going to a dig site tomorrow where mummies and tomb robbers still exist? Just like in the movies?"

"Well, not exactly. Tell ed-Daba is—"

"Splendid!" she barged in. "This trip is due for a little excitement. Oh, I've always wanted to explore the secret passages in those enormous old pyramids and stand on the big stone paws of that giant Stinks."

"Sphinx."

"Right. Not those common little statues, mind you—but the granddaddy of them all—the Big Stinks."

Elliot tugged the brim of his hat forward over one eye.

"One small problem. The pyramids and Giant 'Stinks' are that way." He pointed to the south end of the museum. "And Tell ed-Daba is that way." His finger led her eyes in the opposite direction.

"Well then . . . what sort of pyramids will we find at this Tell-a-Llama dig?"

"Tell ed-Daba," he repeated slowly. "It means 'Mound of the Hyena.'"

Her expression soured. "Now *there's* a pleasant thought."

"We won't find any pyramids there," Elliot continued. "It's not usually thought of as a burial dig site for royalty—which is why I'm surprised this mummy showed up there."

"Why are we going there if there are no pyramids?" She asked, groaning with irritation. Before Elliot could muster an answer, she stopped him. "Don't tell me, I know. Uncle Mason wishes to sift around for old pots of some sort, doesn't he?"

"Uh . . . something like that," came his sheepish reply.

"I knew it! Why doesn't he add a bit of zing to these globe-trotting travels of ours? When there are pyramids, he looks for pots. When there are bones, he looks for bronze. Just once I'd like to drop in on a dig site and find more than dust."

"All discoveries are important," Elliot defended, "and exciting."

"For you, perhaps. Of course, your idea of excitement is watching ice melt. Me? I'm ready for adventure." She tapped again on the lid of the glass case and spoke to the mummy's remains. "Are you with me, old girl?"

A female voice answered, making Rachel's knees wobble, and her head feel woozy.

"Yes, Rachel . . . I am."

Rachel caught her breath and refused to let it go.

"Your name is Rachel, is it not?" the voice persisted.

Her hands trembled. She gazed first at the mummy. It hadn't moved an inch. Next she glanced into Elliot's eyes for help, but found him staring blankly over her shoulder. With one swift motion she whirled around.

"And this must be Elliot," the voice concluded. The girl behind the voice offered an outstretched hand to Rachel, who shook it after a moment's hesitation. "My father said I might find you here."

Elliot grinned ear to ear.

"Well, your father was right." Clearly, he was happy as a Mummy's Uncle to have been found by this Egyptian girl.

"Who is your father exactly?" Rachel said rather coldly. She didn't appreciate being scared half out of her wits by someone sneaking up behind her, especially by a slightly taller, slightly older, bronze-skinned girl with dancing eyes the color of chocolate drops.

"Dr. Ahmed, from the University. He spoke at the conference this morning."

"Not about obelisks, I trust," Rachel huffed.

"No, he spoke about juglet pottery from the Delta

regions," Elliot jumped in. "I enjoyed his talk very much."

"Thank you," the girl answered politely. Elliot shook her hand—several times—prompting the archeologist's daughter to introduce herself. "I am Kasha."

"Is that a traditional name?" Elliot asked. "Like the city, Akasha?"

"No." She smiled. "Actually my real name is one you might find difficult to pronounce. My youngest sister cannot pronounce it, so she calls me Kasha. So do all of my friends."

"It's great meeting you," Elliot beamed. He shook her hand again.

"Didn't you already do that?" Rachel pointed out.

"My father knows your father . . . your uncle," Kasha added, including Rachel in their conversation. "I suppose he thought it would be good for us to meet. There are very few young people attending the conference."

"Two. Make that three, now," Rachel interrupted.

Kasha laughed kindly. "I think you are right. But it is a puzzle to me why more young people do not take advantage of such an opportunity. As you were saying, I believe all of archeology should be exciting and adventurous, don't you?" She was addressing Elliot, who appeared hypnotized by this girl's wavy hair that cascaded down her back like a river of black pearls. He stammered out an answer.

"I feel the same way," he echoed.

Rachel rolled her eyes in disgust.

"So, are you enjoying the museum?" Kasha inquired.

"It's great," Elliot said, no longer tongue-tied. "I was here once before, a long time ago. The artifacts are amazing, but it's the mummies that fascinate me. I love them. I could spend days here."

"He nearly *ended* our days here," Rachel perked up. She casually stepped between her Mummy King cousin and the Egyptian girl with the fancy nickname. "The glass box there began to buckle," she explained, "while Elliot was trying to impress that tour group behind us. Fortunately we were able to save the exhibit before disaster struck."

The girl's wide, round eyes grew even wider.

Elliot threw Rachel a straight look before quickly changing the subject. "We did find something interesting. Maybe you can help us out." He fished in his vest pocket to reclaim the gold half-moon artifact that had clinked at Rachel's feet minutes earlier. He held it out to her. "Any clue as to what it might be?"

Kasha rolled the crafted gold in the palm of her hand.

"Did you notice the symbols on the rounded surface?"

Elliot patted his vest. "Got a pencil imprint right here."

"Oh, what a wise thing to do! Where did you find this?"

"Right where you are standing." Rachel pointed at the girl's tennis shoes, poking from beneath her brand new jeans. "It dropped from the display case when I . . . when we were discussing the mummies."

"I need to give it to someone here at the museum," said Elliot.

Already the girl was nodding slowly. She left them for a moment, gold artifact in hand, and approached a uniformed man near the guided tour group. Calling him by name, she held out the item and appeared to give him clear instructions in Egyptian. He accepted the gold piece, then disappeared through an arched doorway.

Elliot took in the whole scene, his mouth slightly open in amazement.

"I'm impressed," he said at last, carefully adjusting his glasses.

"You're *impaired*!" Rachel commented.

Kasha returned to their side.

"We will see that the artifact is prepared and matched to the display," she informed them.

"We?" Elliot's neck stretched to look like that of a mummy—chicken-style. "You mean you're a curator here at the museum?"

She hid a smile. "Just for the summer, until I return to school."

"Wow!" He threw a glance to Rachel. "Did you hear that? I'd give anything to work in this place!"

"Sure," Rachel replied curtly. She sized up their new acquaintance. Obviously this girl and Elliot had much in common—a love of digging up pots and knowing everything, for starters. If Rachel planned to be part of their little group, she would have to act swiftly.

"Come. I will show you the rest of the museum," Kasha offered.

Rachel fell in behind her, leaving Elliot to make a few final mummy notes in his journal.

"So . . . you say you missed the obelisk talk," Rachel remarked. "How unfortunate. I quite enjoyed it."

Kasha gave her a kind but knowing wink.

"Yes. Actually, I think I prefer mine boiled."

CHAPTER 4

"You didn't have to invite them," Rachel snapped the next morning.

"Invite *them*?" Elliot replied. "Actually, they're the ones who invited *us*. Dad and Dr. Ahmed discussed the trip to Tell ed-Daba before we ever arrived in Cairo."

"That's what *she* told you."

"Look," he went on, "Dr. Ahmed arranged our visit to Tell ed-Daba. He's done a lot of work in that area. It seemed only proper to invite him and his daughter along." Carefully, Elliot checked himself in the hotel's mirrored hallway and slicked back his hair before snugging on his dig hat. Moments later the *Ding!* of the elevator signaled that their ride had arrived. Elliot threw his satchel over one shoulder and pulled his suitcase through the doors as they opened. Rachel dragged her suitcase in as well, just as the doors closed. Together they stood in silence, along with five or six other hotel guests, watching the lighted panel above the doors click off the floor numbers passing by. Finally Elliot spoke.

"Dad said he would meet us at the check-out desk."

"I don't trust her."

"Goodness Agnes, Rachel! What are you talking about?"

"You know who I'm talking about. I'm talking about that teenage sphinx who gave us the museum tour last afternoon."

"Kasha is a very smart girl. I sure hope she and her father will accompany us to the dig—we could learn a lot . . . "

"She looks like all of those statues in the main museum area, the ones with big black-and-white eyes."

Elliot adjusted his glasses but said nothing. Shuffling feet reminded Rachel that they were not alone in the elevator. She wasn't one to let opportunity pass her by. Leaning her suitcase against the elevator wall, she turned to address the small, captive audience.

"He's invited two guests to join us on our field trip, one of whom is a snooty teenage girl," Rachel explained to the shocked elevator riders. "And when I say she looks like a statue . . . what I really mean is . . . " Rachel paused to catch her breath as the elevator doors opened onto the lobby, "I think she looks like King Tut." She grabbed her suitcase, swung around, and came eye-to-eye with an enormous pair of black-and-white King Tut eyes standing in the lobby—Kasha's eyes.

"Hi, Kasha," Elliot sang out. He stepped around Rachel, bumping her accidentally with his satchel as he passed. "I didn't expect to see you here this morning."

"Right," Rachel mumbled beneath her breath. "That's

why he's spent the last hour combing his hair."

"I hoped to see you both before you left Cairo," Kasha began. "My father has been asked to address a group of archeologists touring the Egyptian Museum later today. I am afraid we cannot accompany you to Tell ed-Daba."

Rachel looked beyond Elliot's disappointed face to see Dr. Ahmed and Uncle Mason standing together near the check-out desk, where they were discussing a map spread out before them on the counter. A set of keys jingled in Uncle Mason's hand.

Kasha pointed out the lobby windows to an odd-looking vehicle parked in front of the hotel. Then she smiled. "It looks as though you will be traveling to the dig site in style."

Rachel was not amused. First of all, she didn't like this black-haired girl or her sphinx eyes. Nor did she appreciate Kasha barging in on their tour yesterday, only to drag them into the back rooms of the museum where Elliot could "Oooo!" and "Ahh!" over the equipment and storage areas. Rachel also hated traveling around foreign countries in scrappy old vehicles like the heap waiting for them out front. Elliot and Uncle Mason seemed to enjoy the thrill of it, seeing each unsafe trip as a challenge to be met. She saw it as foolishness. The only good news was that Kasha wouldn't be going with them to the dig. For Rachel, that was good news indeed.

"Have you been north of Cairo?" Kasha asked.

"Once," Elliot replied. "But that was a long time ago. I really don't remember." He shifted his weight from one foot to the other as if trying to stand a bit taller. His well-worn hat did make him look a little bigger, and less civilized, as far as Rachel was concerned. Elliot continued, "I imagine you go there often with your father."

"Occasionally. I enjoy the trip, although we usually travel by helicopter."

Rachel rolled her eyes, allowing only Elliot to see.

"By helicopter?" Rachel asked. "Do you carry a flight attendant with you as well?" She tried to hide her remark with a courteous voice, but it came out sounding slightly rude. A poke to her ribs from Elliot's satchel bag confirmed that she had made her point. To him, at least.

"No," Kasha offered a gracious smile. "But that is a good idea. Perhaps you can suggest it to my father."

Uncle Mason motioned them toward the hotel's front doors with a jingle of the keys. Then he and Dr. Ahmed shook hands and parted.

"I really wish you were coming along," Elliot gushed. "A guided tour around the dig would be great."

"I am sure you will make your own tours. Who knows? You may find that adventure we all wish for."

Rachel said a brief, impersonal goodbye and dragged her suitcase toward the door. Elliot followed, but only after spending an extra minute or two with Sphinx Woman. By the time he joined Rachel and Uncle Mason, most of their travel bags were crammed into the vehicle.

"Well!" he said cheerily. "I guess we should load and be on our way."

"Bit late for that," Rachel snapped. "Your father and I

have done all the loading, in case you hadn't noticed. All but *your* bags, that is. Perhaps those gaga eyes of yours don't see clearly."

"Okay . . . let's see if my stuff fits into the Land Rover," Elliot directed.

"Land Rover? That's what you call this box on wheels? I'd call this heap a land-*over*. I'm certain it has landed over on its side many times!"

Elliot lifted the rear cargo door.

"I think there's room," he said. "If you don't mind holding an equipment bag on your lap, that is."

"I do mind! I mind terribly much! *You* should be holding it."

He loaded the last suitcase and quickly pulled the door into locking position, before everything could tumble out the back. "One of us holds the equipment bag; one of us shares a seat with the pickax and hand shovel. Your choice."

"I choose to fly home to Kentucky."

"Here," Elliot called out, tossing her a large candy bar and a winning smile. "A going away gift from Kasha." He also had one in his hand. "Don't worry, I thanked her for both of us."

Chocolate with almonds—or at least an Egyptian version of chocolate with almonds. One of Rachel's favorites.

"Kasha says it's one of her favorites," he tacked on.

Silently she slipped the bar into her waist pack for temporary safekeeping. She then boarded the Land Rover. It looked like a giant square bug on wheels, with white folded wings on top, a dark underbelly, and a pair of round headlight eyes. A large splash of dried mud decorated the passenger door. Probably left over from the crash that killed the last people riding in it, Rachel thought.

She took her place next to the pickax and settled in for the three-hour trip. Uncle Mason bounced behind the steering wheel, turned over the starter, and raced the engine. As he pulled from the hotel's circular drive the hand shovel shifted, bonking Rachel squarely on her knee.

"Ouch! Why must we carry all of this bother?" she lashed out.

Uncle Mason answered, his eyes glued to the jammed Cairo traffic. "Dr. Ahmed needed supplies dropped at Tell ed-Daba. Seems the least we could do since he rounded up this Rover for us to use the next few days."

So it was Kasha's father who had provided this ghastly vehicle for their traveling pleasure. Perhaps he and his daughter didn't intend for them to reach the dig alive.

"The Rover is Dr. Ahmed's own personal vehicle," continued Uncle Mason. "Quite good of him to let us borrow it like this, don't you think?"

Elliot nodded heartily. But Rachel refused to answer her uncle's slanted question. She knew very few people who would give candy bars and Land Rovers to near strangers. There had to be a catch.

The next two hours clocked miles of travel, from the bustling streets and tall buildings of Egypt's capital city through outlying settlements and thriving croplands.

This luxury Land Rover of Kasha's didn't come with air conditioning, so the three travelers had firsthand exposure to the sounds and smells of northern Egypt through the open Rover windows. The road north followed the fertile Nile River Valley. On either side of the river, lush fields of green and brown formed a colorful border between the river and the vast stretches of desert surrounding it. Unfortunately, Elliot did a lot of reading aloud during the trip. He pointed out unimportant landmarks and rattled off names of places Rachel forgot the moment he said them. As they left the main river and followed along its northeastern branch, Elliot began to blab about the obelisks of Tanis that lay beyond their destination. Rachel ended that little talk by showing him the hand shovel and offering to do major damage to his hat—and anything beneath it if he continued to share his know-it-all information.

The last thirty minutes of the ride were quite uncomfortable. Rachel's ears grew tired of the constant whistling of the wind, and the heat made sweating a full-time job. Finally, as they rolled along an asphalt road beside a narrow canal, a settlement appeared.

"There it is," Elliot said excitedly. He sat up in his seat as Uncle Mason slowed the Rover to turn off the paved highway.

In the distance, lay neatly-fitted tiles of land. The large blocks formed a series of crossword puzzle squares, some covered by green crops, others plowed and empty. Narrow stretches of dirt or water divided one field from another. Beyond the farmland stood lines of trees surrounding the Tell ed-Daba dig site, forming a distinct border between the land and the sky. Their feathery branches swayed in the breeze. An occasional palm tree loomed among the tree borders, each with a circle of deep green palm leaves bursting from its top like exploding fireworks.

Uncle Mason followed the road that bridged across the blue-gray water of the calm canal. Past the cropland a collection of mudbrick buildings were scattered between fields. Except for the palm trees, Rachel was reminded of the flat, open prairies and sod houses she had read about in American history at school. Many of the mudbrick buildings had flat roofs covered in straw. Local villagers were repairing several of them under the watchful eye of an occasional sheep or pair of cattle.

"You didn't tell me we were visiting the theme park for 'Little House on the Prairie,'" Rachel moaned. This place had "boring" written all over it. First three days of stuffy hotel, now three days of heat, dust, and mudbrick houses with livestock in the front yards. She sighed loudly. "Why must all of these places we visit consist of nothing more than . . ." She squinted over Uncle Mason's hat at the activity near the dig itself. ". . . Nothing more than dirt, and rocks, and strange people speaking languages no one understands!" she finally finished.

Uncle Mason stroked his gray beard and answered her with a chuckle. "I'm sure they understand each other quite well. But that's part of the fun, isn't it? Learning about new cultures, new people, new places. It's the journey in life that's interesting, Rachel. The destination isn't always so important."

Rachel had to agree. Nothing about Tell ed-Daba seemed important to her.

"Oh, perhaps I shall appreciate all of this bother someday when I'm terribly old—too old to care. Perhaps when I'm thirty years old or so."

A new chuckle rumbled from Uncle Mason's broad chest. He meant well—Rachel knew that. And he had a heart of gold, always willing to include her when Mother simply dropped her at his doorstep. Elliot meant well, too, although he really could be a royal pain in the neck sometimes.

"I don't suppose they have entertainment . . . you know, a movie theatre, video arcade, things of that sort," Rachel wondered aloud. No one spoke, so she answered her own inquiry. "No, I suppose not."

A handful of young children in brightly colored clothing began to crowd around the Rover as it moved slowly past the first set of buildings.

"This is the village," explained Uncle Mason. "The Tell is on up past the road's end."

Rachel looked into the smiling faces of the children who were calling out to them and waving their hands in greeting.

"You would think they had never seen a car before," she said flatly.

Elliot laughed and hung his hand out the window to return the village greeting. Then he called to Rachel over his shoulder.

"Maybe they just love Land Rovers!"

"Jolly good!" she called back. "Let's give them this one!"

"There's the mission site!" Uncle Mason exclaimed over the noise. "That's Tell ed-Daba."

Elliot pressed his free hand to his hat and leaned halfway out the car window.

"I think I've died and gone to heaven," he murmured.

CHAPTER 5

Rachel scanned the flat horizon, the sandy soil, and the rough gray patches of scrubby bushes scattered about. Elliot had to be confused.

"This is your idea of heaven? You must be joking! Your brain has cooked under that awful hat of yours in three hours of no air conditioning. All I see is hot dust and sweaty people wearing long robes in 4,000 degree weather."

A dozen local workers, many dressed in ankle-length wrap-around robes, milled about the mudbrick walls of the dig site. They climbed in and out of sunken rooms on short earthen ramps. Tarps were strung over the dig area to shade the workers from the blazing sun. Women balanced baskets of soil and artifacts on their shawl-covered heads. The pace was slow but steady, no doubt in response to the heat.

"This may be one of the most active dig sites in all of Egypt right now," Elliot countered. "You can almost smell the history pouring from the ground."

"Correction. You can smell the heat pouring from

these people! Did someone forget to tell them it is summer? They must be planning a snow skiing trip after dinner with those clothes!"

"In the desert, sometimes it's cooler to dress warmer," Elliot said, " . . . if that makes any sense."

"It doesn't." Rachel had seen her share of excavation sites, having traveled halfway around the world with Elliot and Uncle Mason a number of times. This site looked frighteningly like all the others: hot, dirty, and boring.

She spotted one of the resident archeologists squatting on an exposed wall giving instructions to two dusty workers. A long sheet of heavy paper lay rolled out before him. Beyond them lay several sets of mudbrick buildings like those they first encountered near the canal. Most were clustered into village groups, although a few stood alone some distance from the excavation area.

"What are those for?" she asked.

"Part of the Austrian mission, I guess. Residences, things like that. The Austrians and locals have worked here together for a long time . . . twenty years or so."

"How sad for them."

"We'll probably be staying in one of the mudbrick complexes on the far side." He motioned toward a bunch of dreary mud buildings with small, square openings for windows, all connected together in the distance.

"How sad for *us*."

It really wasn't as sad as Rachel made it out to be. She knew that. In fact, the occasional spattering of palm trees striping the horizon reminded her a little of the Florida coast—or at least what she had seen of it on a whirlwind business trip with Mother two years ago. Croplands much like those bordering the Nile River continued into this Delta area where canals replaced the big river as a source of water. Other than heat and boredom, this might not be a bad place for a two-day vacation—provided she had a few minor items like a swimming pool, a miniature golf course, and a shopping mall.

After circling the site and dodging low mounds of dirt and clumps of brush, Uncle Mason bounced the Land Rover to a stop. Silently he surveyed the excavations while the dust cloud created by the rover slowly settled around them.

"Well?" Rachel finally spoke up. "What are you waiting for? Pile out, then." She turned to Elliot. "I know *you're* itching to get out there and dig around. Perhaps you'll dig up a life-size stone hippo or something."

Elliot and Uncle Mason both grabbed their shoulder bags. Then Uncle Mason spoke.

"We've only got two days at this dig—three at the most. So let's make the most of it. If we all work together, we can contribute a great deal to the Austrians' efforts here. And the SIMA museum will benefit as well. The Austrians graciously offered to let us take any artifacts we uncover back to the States for extended study."

"That's great!" Elliot piped up.

"Finders keepers?" Rachel perked up. "Really?"

"Well, within reason," cautioned Uncle Mason. "The

Egyptian government reserves the right to keep any artifacts it wishes. This is their country, after all. We're simply visitors."

"So, you're telling me, " Rachel felt her excitement level begin to surge, "that if I find a mummy, I can keep it?"

Her uncle let out a laugh as he climbed from the Land Rover, bag in hand.

"We'll cross that tomb when we come to it," he joked.

"That reminds me . . ." Rachel began. She handed Elliot her all-purpose waist pack. Dutifully, he cinched it over one shoulder while burdening the other with his own satchel bag. "What did the mummy say when he chopped down the tree? . . . *Tomb*-ber!" she answered herself.

A smile lurked beneath Uncle Mason's bearded chin.

"Too many riddle books for you, my dear," he quipped. He opened the back of the Rover to examine their gear. "We'll leave all of our personal bags packed for now and unload them later at the dig house. Let's go meet our hosts."

Rachel fell in behind Uncle Mason and Elliot for the short hike to the dig itself. Before they reached the short, exposed walls of the dig, a middle-aged archeologist came out to greet them. Uncle Mason introduced himself, Rachel, and Elliot, then immediately set to work with his new colleague, unrolling a large paper bearing a diagram of the excavation. Elliot peeked between the two men at the dig plans, absorbing it all like a sponge. Several hot, sunny minutes later Rachel gave him a poke in the ribs.

"What are we supposed to do now?" she asked impatiently.

Elliot barely took his eyes from the plans.

"Once we learn the dig layout we'll help with excavation work."

Rachel glanced down into the large, square pits carved two meters deep.

"You mean we go down there, scrape up dirt, and carry it back up here? All day?"

He didn't answer. Their Austrian host had moved onto the second plan and had Elliot's full attention again. Slowly Rachel backed away from the group of dirt-diggers. She strayed beyond the first excavation site to a forgotten dirt pile. Apparently this was one of the places workers dumped their baskets of soil. From here she watched the colorful lines of robes and baskets making their way up and down the paths leading from the square pits.

"I did not come here to do slave labor," she grumbled. She wiggled her fingers through her hair and pulled it back away from her cheek. Her shadow barely shaded her own feet from the high midday sun. "I've been sent here to die. The only question remaining is, 'Which will kill me first—the heat or the boredom?'"

A deep sigh accompanied her to the base of a palm tree where she sat cross-legged.

"Ouch!"

A sharp stab awakened her rear end. Popping to her feet, she whirled around to see what had attacked her backside.

"Decide to do some jumping jacks?" Elliot stood in front of her, arms crossed, glasses already adjusted on his nose. She clenched her teeth.

"All right, then! What did you poke me with?"

His face retained its usual, innocent expression, and he uncrossed his arms as if to lend a helping hand.

"What are you talking about?"

Immediately she knew he was telling the truth. Honesty was always a safe bet with Elliot.

"Something jabbed me," Rachel mumbled with a kick into the loose brush around the base of the tree. A tiny bead of gold appeared amid the dirt and overgrowth. Another kick exposed the object poking from the soil. Her cousin went to one knee for a better look.

"Hmmmm."

"Don't just squat there, singing to it! Pull it out— unless you intend to sit on it yourself!" She moved around him, reached through the brush, and gave the thing a jerk. It nudged the surface but didn't break free. She tugged harder a second time and the gold stick lifted from the tangled growth. With it came a knob of gold the size of her fist. As it twisted beneath her fingers, Rachel became keenly aware of what she held. The distinct shape of an enormous bug dangled at the base of the stick.

"Yuk!" The heavy, gold artifact practically flew from her fist as she flung it away.

"Goodness Agnes!" Elliot exclaimed. "It's a scarab!" He scrambled to retrieve it.

"It looks like a bug statue to me . . . a big, ugly bug."

"Scarabs *are* bugs," Elliot answered, returning to the base of the tree with the artifact in his hands. "Beetles, to be exact. This statue appears to be made from a mixture of gold and some other metal." He glanced up at her through his wire-rimmed glasses. "You know those fat, black beetles that jump against your screen door on summer nights?"

"June bugs?" Rachel replied, still slightly shaken by the experience of pulling a gold bug statue from the ground.

"Well, they're one type of scarab. Anyway, ancient Egyptians used to worship certain scarab beetles."

Rachel gingerly touched the golden ornament, careful not to leave her finger on it for too long. "Worship bugs? You've simply made that up, haven't you?"

"Nope," Elliot answered. "They worshiped lots of things. Crocodiles, cats, hippopotami . . ."

"I suppose I could worship a hippo," she broke in thoughtfully, "if he were little and cute. But a bug? I think not."

"Back 3,000 years ago Egyptians believed scarabs— dung beetles, actually—had special powers."

Rachel felt her face twist into a grimace. "Dung beetles? That's disgusting! What sorts of powers could bugs living in sheep droppings possess?"

"Oh, just the basic stuff . . . power over sunrise and sunset, everlasting life. No big deal." Elliot smiled slyly. "Doesn't look like this particular bug had much power over anything, though. He's missing a leg and part of one wing. But it's amazing you found it."

"I assume you are going somewhere with this twisted little tale of yours," Rachel surrendered. "Other than making me ill."

Elliot settled back into that "ready to lecture" pose of his, the one that made him look ever so much like Uncle Mason.

"Dung beetles live in . . . well, in animal droppings, right?"

"You're the one who seems to know all about them. I'll take your word for it, thank you."

"So, if you're an ancient Egyptian who always sees living beetles crawling out of dead droppings, you just assume they are reborn, over and over again. Life from death. Everlasting life." Elliot tilted the gold bug on its head and slowly moved it backwards. "They also held traditional beliefs that a giant dung beetle walked backwards across the sky each day, rolling the sun as it went, like an enormous yellow ball."

"Lovely. I really don't need to hear all of this."

"Sure you do. The only way to understand an archeological find is to understand the culture it came from. Like a window into time." He smiled to himself. "I like that—'a window into time'—that's almost as good as your 'saving the past for your future' TV ad."

"Oh, cork it, will you?" She offered him a wag of her finger as warning. "I don't want to hear another word about dung windows or time beetles or everlasting telly ads."

Elliot had already moved on, lost in thought as usual. He walked up a gently sloping mound some distance from the actual excavations to a spot with a better view. She followed behind him, blocking the stubborn summer sunlight from her face with her forearm. When he reached the mound's crest he turned to her.

"Looks like you could use a trusty dig hat . . . want to borrow mine?"

"No."

"It's only going to get hotter out here. A sunburned scalp hurts for days."

"I wouldn't be caught dead in a hat like that," Rachel informed him.

Elliot grinned and nodded.

"Okay," he said in a voice edged with warning. "But when your head feels like a roasted marshmallow, just let me know. I've got an extra hat."

"I seriously doubt that your hats would fit me . . . I don't wear a size P like you do." She watched his puzzled reaction then waited several seconds before finishing. "P . . . for 'pea-brain.'"

He simply shook his head, slipped the satchel from his shoulder and sat on a small boulder that lay half-buried in the soil. He put the golden beetle statue on a nearby rock to examine it. Rachel stared the bug straight in the eyes—at least she *thought* it was the eyes—while rolling Elliot's freaky scarab facts over and over in her mind. Then she turned to him.

"I say we bury the ridiculous thing back where we found it."

"You're joking, right?" Elliot held the bug figure inches from his face. "It's a good find. Actually, scarab ornaments should be fairly common here. The Hyksos—the people who once lived here—used them for decorations. And jewelry."

"No wonder they died out . . . they worshiped bugs."

"They also ruled this part of Egypt for several hundred years." He plucked a small strip of cloth from his satchel and began wrapping the artifact, probably for safe transport to some museum.

"Wait," Rachel crowed. "I do believe there's something tucked into this blasted bug." She reached across Elliot's vest and fished inside his satchel for a pencil. She then jabbed its tip into the hollow gold beetle statue in Elliot's hand. "Paper, perhaps. Or cloth possibly, I can't really tell." Careful not to touch the hideous insect unless absolutely necessary, she prodded inside the scarab until she hooked the object. She dragged it to the opening in the statue's back like a skilled surgeon and, in the process, found herself toiling over her work like—dare she say it—an archeologist.

"I can't believe I'm doing this," she mumbled as she plucked at the wad of material. "Scraping crud from inside some old bug statue we've just dug up. Mother always warned me not to play with things I found on the ground. I must say, she deserves some credit for that tidbit of wisdom."

She thought she heard Elliot chuckle.

"It isn't the least bit funny," she went on. "No telling what sorts of germs one could pick up from this activity." In her impatience she finally thrust her thumb and forefinger into the artifact, pinched the wad between them, and yanked it out. "No telling at all. Diseases, parasites . . ."

"Body parts," Elliot added calmly.

"Body parts? Where on earth did you get that disgusting idea?"

"Oh, I don't know. I guess from that thumb . . . the one you're holding in your hand, I mean."

CHAPTER 6

The muffled sound of shoes sneaking across a mud-brick floor and into her sleeping room froze Rachel's breath in her throat. She felt her eyes grow wide and her heart pound wildly. Slowly the sound drew closer, accompanied by the faint rustling of clothes moving in the darkness. A presence approached her bedside then stopped, and a soft hiss of breath hung in the black air. She tensed her shoulders around her neck in fear. Then a cloaked whisper fell into the room.

"Rachel. Rachel, are you asleep?" It was Elliot.

"You Jello-brain!" she growled in a coarse whisper, slamming her covers against the wall with an angry thud. "What on earth are you doing! You nearly scared me to death!" Her chest still pounded like a bass drum in a marching band.

"Sorry. I just wondered if you were asleep yet."

"Yes! I'm asleep! Can't you hear me snoring?" She could barely make out Elliot's shape in the dim moonlight cast through her small square window. He had on his hat. "I'm talking in my sleep right now. And any moment I shall sleepwalk over to where you are standing and pop you!"

Elliot laughed in the darkness. "I figured you were still awake."

"Of course I'm awake. It isn't every day a person finds a chopped-off body part in her hands." The memory of their afternoon discoveries at the dig hung in her mind. "I don't dare doze off for dreaming about mummy thumbs in dirty gold bugs."

"I can't sleep either." Her cot creaked as Elliot sat at the foot of the bed. "I did a little reading after supper. And I took a walk around the excavation site past some of the outbuildings at the far edge of the dig. I'd like to go back and check something out. But I could use your help."

Rachel sat straight up. "If you need me, it must be something important, something that requires great intelligence . . . something grand and glorious and . . ."

"It's snooping."

"It's what?"

"Snooping." His voice trailed off. ". . . Well, sort of."

"Well now, that's certainly an unusual request from Mr. Mind-His-Own-Business."

"It won't take long . . . ten, fifteen minutes at the most."

"Tonight? It's dark out there."

"Exactly. That's why we need to go now."

It wasn't often Elliot asked for her help. He rarely asked for anyone's help, including Uncle Mason's. Snooping at Elliot's request was an offer too good to pass up.

"What time is it?" she inquired.

"Still early, really." He pushed one of the half-dozen buttons on his space-age watch. A blue-green light glowed in the darkness. "It's only half past ten." He released the button and the light disappeared. "One of the Austrian archeologists has an electric generator set up near the dig site. They're doing some night work. I imagine Dad's out there, too."

"What, exactly, do you . . . do *we* intend to do?" She thought she heard him smile.

"Nothing much. Pull on you shoes. I'll explain on the way."

"Oh, all right! This had better be good." Still dressed, she flopped her feet to the floor and began putting on her shoes. Suddenly a frightful thought struck her. "This hasn't anything to do with that little incident earlier today, has it? The one involving the mummy appendage?" She was certain she heard her cousin smile this time.

"Come on."

Elliot's shadowy outline led her from the sleeping room, down the short hallway, and out into the starry night. A light breeze greeted them. Five minutes later they had walked past several smaller excavations and a cluster of mudbrick houses. The glare of light bulbs and the sputter of a generator rose up to meet them at the edge of a mound. A handful of workers and two dirt-diggers, including Uncle Mason, sat at the edge of the dig site with their noses buried in a basket.

"They found a bronze axe head at dusk," Elliot explained. "Since we've only got a couple of days, Dad talked them into a night dig. He's pretty excited."

"An axe head . . . of course. I'd be turning cart-wheels," she jeered.

Elliot ignored her—he had become quite good at that—and continued on, away from the lighted site. He took a flashlight from his bag and they traced a path toward a lone mudbrick outbuilding which sat between two small hills overgrown with short palms. He stretched out his hand to halt her, clicked off the flashlight and knelt near a bunchy palm. Rachel did the same. In the distance behind them, faint voices echoed from the lighted dig. Otherwise, the night remained silent.

Nearly a minute passed before Elliot adjusted his hat, checked the time on his watch, and stood.

"Okay," he said simply. "Let's head back home."

Rachel felt her mouth drop open.

"Oh, no you don't," she threatened softly. "I didn't put on shoes, hike in the dark, and squat by some old mud hut for nothing. I thought we were going snooping!"

"We just did."

"You call this snooping? No wonder you asked me along. You don't even know what snooping is." She searched for his eyes in the darkness. "What in blazes are we doing out here?"

"Confirming a hunch." He nodded toward the build-ing. "Do you see anyone in there?"

"Don't be ridiculous. It's pitch black in there."

"Right. It's empty. Most of the mud structures have people in them at night. Not this one."

"Maybe the people in this mud shack are doing what I should be doing . . . sleeping!"

"Nope. It's empty. Not only that, it is new. It's got

metal rods built into the structure for strength and its got a locked door. And there's an obelisk leaned against one wall." He pulled out his flashlight and turned toward their sleeping quarters.

"Uggghhh! Obelisks again! I don't care if I never . . ." Elliot's flashlight beam had already disappeared behind one of the mounds. She chased after him, nearly tripping over a palm clump in the darkness. Finally she grabbed his vest, forcing him to stop.

"What's this got to do with mummy parts? Or with me, for that matter?"

"Well, it might just explain why mummies were found here in the first place. And as for you . . . I thought you liked your archeology mixed with a touch of adventure."

"Why do I get the feeling I'm about to hear a lecture?" she said with a sigh. She drew a second deep breath. "All right, Mr. Indiana Jones. Out with it."

Side by side, they trekked back to the Austrian mudbrick mission house as Elliot explained his hunch.

"Remember when we discussed the Nile Delta region on the drive here this afternoon?" he reminded her.

"Discussion? I don't recall saying much. I do remember you flapping on about it for quite some time, however."

"I wouldn't expect to find any stone obelisks here at Tell ed-Daba . . . certainly not leaned against newly-built mudbrick flathouses. According to Kasha's father, most of them are found farther north by the ruins of Tanis."

"And since *she* is perfect, we both know Kasha's father could never be wrong," she jumped in.

"So . . ." he continued, ignoring her remark as he sidestepped a clump of low brush in their path, "you don't just 'misplace' an obelisk. They're too big and heavy. Someone put it here. What we've got so far is a stolen obelisk, a new 'old' outbuilding, and a mummy's thumb."

"And a broken gold bug," she added.

Elliot stopped dead in his tracks. Grasping his satchel under his arm, he bolted forward toward the outline of mission buildings lying ahead, nearly losing his hat in the process.

"That's it . . . that's it!" he called out over his shoulder. The beam of his flashlight bounced wildly as he ran. "Come on!"

"Wait!" hollered Rachel. "You're the only one with a blasted flashlight!" She watched him run the last hundred meters to the mission house, leaving her to find her way in the dim moonlight.

In the three or four minutes it took to stumble to the mission, Rachel managed to work up a bit of a temper. She burst into the mudbrick mission house where Elliot had lit a lantern and was now calmly unzipping his satchel.

"Hyenas!" she croaked loudly.

"Shhhh! You might disturb the others."

"The other whats? The other hyenas? For your information, I've been blundering about in the dark, in the wilderness, no doubt under the watchful eye of crazed animals living out there on Hyena Mound, or whatever it is you call this place. I once read that a pack of hyenas can tear a man to pieces in minutes. Without my

keen sense of direction I'd still be out there. Hyena
chow. By morning there would be nothing left of me
but hair and shoelaces!"

"Let me show you what I've figured . . ." Elliot started, ignoring her frenzy.

She grabbed his hat and spun him around by the
head before he could finish.

"Did you hear me? I've been looking death in the
face and you're in here zipping bags!"

"Okay," he apologized. "I got a little carried away. But
an idea struck me and I just had to check it out. I never
meant to leave you out there, Rachel."

"Next time it shall be more than an idea striking you,
and the *hyenas* will carry you away!"

"Now can I show you what I've figured out?"

"Do I have a choice?" She flopped into the chair next
to his. He had apologized, as usual.

Elliot drew his chair closer to the flickering lantern.
Then, fumbling in his vest pocket, he retrieved the
paper bearing the imprint he had made yesterday in the
museum. Rachel watched as he adjusted his glasses and
studied the pencil image with its Egyptian markings.

"You know, I should have recognized this from the
start." He traced the outline surrounding the markings
with his finger. "At first I thought the gold crescent we
found at the museum yesterday was the official seal of
that female mummy. But it isn't." He raised the paper
and turned the image in her direction. "Look familiar
to you?"

"It looks exactly like an imprint of the gold chunk we
found under the mummy case," she sneered, hoping to

make his question seem foolish by giving him an obvious answer.

"Think 'bug,'" Elliot grinned. He slipped his hand into his satchel and brought out the cloth-wrapped scarab. "Better yet . . . think 'broken bug.'" Carefully he unwrapped the one-winged beetle with the dried mummy's thumb left just where they had found it—inside the gold insect statue.

"I can't believe you've carried that disgusting thumb around with you all day," she observed.

"Rachel . . . that gold crescent we found is the missing wing from this scarab statue! Look!" He laid the paper imprint atop the gold artifact. Sure enough, it lined up perfectly.

"Here, let me see that," Rachel said, squinting at the paper in the lantern light.

The tiny etchings in the tracing were stacked like an Indian totem pole, one upon the other, six in all. Two resembled miniature boat oars standing paddle-side up. One was a square, one a circle decorated like a striped ball, one looked like waves on the ocean, and the final symbol was that used in every mummy movie she had ever watched—the open-headed cross representing eternal life.

"I need to translate those hieroglyphic symbols," he said almost to himself. "It's a name of some kind . . . a person's name."

"How do you know it is a name?" she wondered.

"See this oval surrounding the symbols? That means it's a proper name."

"So . . . this person's name would be . . ." She looked

again at the hieroglyphic images, "Mr. Beach-ball Boat-Head-Who-Lives-Forever. What a coincidence. I know three other people with that name!" She laughed out loud at her own attempt at a joke.

"You know what this *really* means, don't you? It means that the scarab belongs to the thumbless mummy in Cairo. And it means that someone removed the thumb, stuck it in the beetle for safekeeping, but for some reason tossed it aside."

"Why would anyone lop off a mummy's thumb, then throw it away?"

"Tomb robbers would be my guess. They probably planned to take the thumb to a potential buyer . . . "

"Buyer? Whatever for?"

"That's one of those 'disgusting' things you don't want me to tell you," Elliot baited her. "Anyway, they must have been taken by surprise somewhere near this dig. I'm betting they threw the beetle into the brush at the base of that palm tree and ran, intending to return for it later. Workers dumped dirt from the excavations there too, burying it deeper."

"I find that whole story a bit hard to swallow, Mr. Sherlock Tombs. However, I also find it worth a snoop or two. You believe that empty mud building we visited tonight is a tomb robber hideout, don't you?"

Even in the dim lantern light, Elliot's teeth shone as he smiled.

"See?" he said. "I knew you were the right person to ask for snooping advice."

CHAPTER 7

Rachel awoke to the low whistle of a tea kettle simmering down the hall. She lay on her back, eyes closed, and listened for the whistle's soft call to grow into a shrill cry, signaling the water was ready for tea. This would be a nice, leisurely morning, she decided. Read the paper, watch the telly, possibly go to the pool later for a cool dip. She snuggled deeper into the bedsheets and opened one eye. In the near darkness, all she could make out was the faint shadow of her own cot on a plain, mudbrick floor. An instant later she remembered yesterday's events and recalled where she was—Egypt, not Kentucky.

Someone removed the kettle from the burner. The aroma of freshly-brewed tea drifted into her sleeping room. The sound of teacups clinking and book pages turning replaced the kettle's whistle. Beyond her window the dig lay dark and silent, awaiting the dawn. Rachel stretched, yawned, and rubbed her itchy eyes.

"What time is it?" she whispered to herself.

"Early." Elliot's lanky form stood at her sleeping

room doorway. She squinted through the dim light for a better view.

"Wait a minute," she mumbled. "I could swear we had this same conversation only hours ago."

"We did."

As her eyes adjusted to the dimness she could make out Elliot's hat, beneath which were a pair of tired, yet lively green eyes. He held three books in his hands. "What are you doing up at this hour? And what time is it, anyway?"

"Reading. And it's five thirty in the morning," he answered.

Rachel let a low groan rumble from her throat and fell back against her pillow.

"How about a cup of hot tea?" Elliot offered.

"I would love a cup of tea." She sat up in her bed. "Why are you up so early?"

"I never really went to bed," he shrugged. "Guess there were too many questions to be answered."

"I've got another question . . . why am *I* up at five thirty?"

He crossed the room and handed her a steaming teacup. "Things will get busy at the dig soon. I'd hoped to do a little detective work before we start our real work at the excavation."

"We? Oh, no no no. Not *we* my dear cousin. *You*." She sipped her first bit of tea. Even on a summer morning, it tasted good. "You may be out there in the dust, digging tunnels in the dirt with hand shovels if you wish. But I shan't be with you. I don't intend to go down into any excavations today . . . or any day."

Elliot pulled a wooden chair from the corner and sat in the darkened room.

"There is more to this dig than I realized," he said.

Rachel purposely slurped her second sip of tea.

"It is a bit too warm, don't you think?"

"Well, sure ... but it's summertime. Egypt is mainly desert so the dig is bound to be hotter ... "

"Not the dig, silly! The tea!"

"Listen, Rachel, it's a privilege to dig here." Elliot's voice had an edge to it. "Besides being the site of several ancient cities, Tell ed-Daba may be the burial place of one of the most famous people in history. Old, old history, that is."

He was sounding too serious for her. So she tried to lighten him up a bit. "Oh, really? Which person? Adam ... or Eve?"

"You're warm. Move forward in time. To Joseph."

Rachel noticed one of the books in his hands was Uncle Mason's Bible. She tried to recall what it said about that particular guy.

"Joseph. I've heard that story before—in one of those Vacation Bible School programs you dragged me to see. His father liked him best so his nasty brothers decided to do him in. Didn't he wear some sort of bathrobe or something?"

"In the Bible School play, maybe. But the real Joseph had a special, fancy robe made especially for him by his father. His brothers were jealous so they plotted to kill him. I just re-read the story this morning. They didn't actually kill him. They just threw him in a well and sold him as a slave to merchants headed for Egypt.

Then they dipped his robe in goat blood and told their father he had been attacked by wild animals."

"You always select such pleasant stories, don't you?" She took another swallow of tea.

"There is a happy ending. Joseph grows up to become Pharaoh's right-hand man in Egypt. He interprets dreams and sets up storehouses of grain to keep the people fed when the crops fail. But in between he had a pretty rough life."

"Oh? Just what do you consider a rough life?"

"Well . . . he was an outsider who lived with the Egyptians, even ruled over them. But he always stayed true to his people and his God. That's not always easy to do." Elliot held the book inches from his face and began to read portions aloud in the last glow of moonlight.

Rachel liked a good story. She settled in with her tea as Elliot read to her about Joseph.

"'Now Israel loved Joseph more than any of his other sons,'" Elliot began, "'because he had been born to him in his old age; and he made a richly ornamented robe for him. When his brothers saw that their father loved Joseph more than any of them, they hated him and could not speak a kind word to him'"

"See?" interrupted Rachel, "I told you those rotten brothers intended to do him in."

Elliot ignored her and went on, reading the exciting parts, and filling in the rest himself.

"'So when Joseph came to his brothers, they stripped him of his beautiful robe and threw him into a cistern. Now the cistern was empty of water.' But they didn't leave him there, they sold him to some travelers who were passing by," Elliot explained. "They got Joseph's robe, killed a goat, and dipped the robe in the blood. Then they took the coat back to their father and told him they had found this robe and wanted him to examine the robe and see if it was his son's."

"His father thought he was dead?" Rachel asked. Elliot nodded. "How awful!"

He went on to read how Joseph was made a slave in Egypt, thrown into prison unfairly, and forgotten about. Rachel was listening so closely, it was as if she had met him and knew just how he felt. Early in the story, he didn't have say-so about anything that happened to him. But by the end, his family came together again and Joseph was in charge of everything in Egypt. That last part, where he controlled everything and everyone, was the part she liked best.

"'So Joseph died at the age of a hundred and ten,'" Elliot read before he closed Uncle Mason's Bible. "'And after they embalmed him, he was placed in a coffin . . . in Egypt.'"

Rachel's teacup was empty. The first rays of sunrise warmed her room through the gray dawn.

"You believe Joseph is buried here at this dig, don't you?" she said.

He removed his glasses briefly to clean them on his shirtsleeve.

"No. The Israelites moved his body later, back to the mountains of Israel where his father owned land." He opened the Bible back up and read again. "'Moses took the bones of Joseph with him because Joseph had made the sons of Israel swear an oath. He had said, 'God will surely come to your aid, and then you must carry my bones up with you from this place.' But I *do* think he was buried here first, at Tell ed-Daba. One of these excavations is thought to be his tomb. I'm sure Dr. Ahmed knows more about it. I just wish he could have come along."

Suddenly a faint thumping sound droned in through the window. The thump became louder and finally turned to a chopping roar. Elliot raced to the window and Rachel followed on his heels.

A little way from the dig a small twister of dust rose from the ground as a helicopter slowly touched down. Two people hopped from the craft amid a swirl of dust and noise. The taller of the two shouted something to the helicopter pilot and with a final wave, the pilot lifted off, swung in a tight circle, and headed the aircraft away from the dig into the rising sun.

"What do you make of all that?" Rachel called to Elliot.

He smiled. "It's Dr. Ahmed. And Kasha."

She threw up her hands.

"Of course! They couldn't simply drive across the canal at midday in some death-rover vehicle. They had to make a grand entrance from the sky at dawn . . . waking everyone from their sleep." She stepped from the window and mumbled, "Too bad they didn't land on an obelisk."

Elliot instantly went into action. He began adjusting everything at once—hat, glasses, dig vest—he even bent to tie a loose shoelace.

"My, Mr. Sleepless Night, you certainly seem chipper all of a sudden," Rachel snorted.

"Somebody needs to welcome them to the dig. And since I'm already up . . ."

"And dressed," she butted in, "you might as well do it, eh?"

He threw his satchel over his shoulder on his way out.

"Coming?" he asked.

"No, I'm not coming. I've always thought it rude to arrive by helicopter before breakfast." She stared out the window as Elliot raced to meet the pair. He met them halfway, first offering a handshake to Dr. Ahmed, then gathering some of their travel bags under his arms.

"I can almost hear them now," Rachel grumbled. She stood straight and tall, pulling her hair back to imitate Kasha. "Oh, thank you, Elliot. It is so wonderful of you to meet us. You should be sleeping." She then adjusted make-believe glasses on her nose as she spoke for Elliot. "No big deal," she shrugged in her lower, Elliot-type voice. "I don't sleep at night anyway. I've just been bothering Rachel." "Rachel? She is still here?" Rachel's Kasha character continued. "Too bad, I was hoping she had become a mummy by now."

Uncle Mason and one of the Austrian archeologists intercepted the trio before they made it to the mission house. From the sounds of it, the visitors had been invited to share breakfast. They were welcomed in and directed toward the cooking area. A minute later Elliot was back, still burdened with travel bags and obviously in a hurry.

"Ready for breakfast?" he crowed, half out of breath. Rachel continued staring out the window.

"No, thank you. I seem to have lost my appetite."

Elliot seemed genuinely disappointed that she would miss the meal.

"Well, if you change your mind, you know where we'll be." He left as quickly as he had come.

Rachel spent a few minutes feeling sorry for herself and blaming Kasha for it. They didn't need her here to show them the digs. They had done quite well without her, in fact, what with finding the isolated outbuilding that was certain to be a robbers' hideout. And the beetle-bug. Kasha would never have found that—she probably wouldn't sit her new blue jeans in the dirt in the first place.

The longer Rachel waited, however, the hungrier she became. Sounds of joking and laughter drifted in from the cooking area. So did the smell of a delicious breakfast. Uncle Mason's booming voice occasionally was heard over the chatter of the others, followed by more laughter. Finally she surrendered. Sooner or later she would have to confront the Sphinx Woman. It might as well be during a meal.

"Yes, quite," Rachel said to her reflection in the small wall mirror. "Why should I miss breakfast because of her?" She grabbed her hairbrush and forcefully shoved it through her uncombed hair.

"Aaahhh! Ow! Ow!" Rachel found herself hopping from foot to foot in response to the pain. Leaning closer to the mirror, she gingerly lifted her hair with her fingers to find a bright pink stripe running the length of her scalp—right where her hair had been parted yesterday.

"Sunburn! I've sunburned my scalp!" she cried, angry with Elliot for warning her and even angrier with herself for letting it happen. Now Elliot could gloat. Why must he always be right?

Taking great care to avoid the sore spots, she attempted to finish her brushing. Then she slipped into Elliot's sleeping room, dug out his extra hat, and grudgingly snugged it over her sizzling scalp.

"I shan't miss breakfast because of him either!" she resolved. One deep breath later she stepped down the hall into the dining area. Uncle Mason spotted her first.

"Well, well," he chuckled. "I see you're ready for a dig!"

"Please . . . come and join us." Dr. Ahmed drew out the empty chair beside his own and patted the seat.

"Good morning," Rachel said smartly. She decided to kill them with apparent kindness.

Kasha waved meekly. "It is good to see you again."

"Yes, you too." Rachel cringed inside as she picked the last piece of toast from the plate. It was burnt. "My . . . you must have had a short night, leaving Cairo before dawn." Kasha and her father nodded.

"We are thankful to have such good hosts," Dr. Ahmed grinned as he opened his hand across the now-bare table. No doubt he was referring to the food Rachel had just missed. She considered thanking Kasha for the candy bar gift of yesterday, then thought better of it when she remembered she had eaten both hers and Elliot's at bedtime. Elliot didn't know that yet, of course.

Kasha leaned forward from across the table.

"Elliot has been telling us all about your discoveries here at the dig site. I knew you would find adventure here." Her gaze fell to Elliot. "A golden scarab with a mummy's thumb inside . . . how extraordinary!"

Rachel's heart sank. In less than ten minutes time Elliot had blabbed their secret discoveries to everyone, including Queen Tut. She threw Elliot a glare but he only returned an innocent smile. Laying her burnt toast aside she dabbed at her unfed mouth with a napkin.

Uncle Mason spoke up. "Well, it won't be getting any cooler out there. Are we ready?"

All of the workers at the table agreed heartily as they rose to gather dig equipment for the long day ahead. Kasha got up with her father but turned to Elliot and Rachel on her way out.

"I would like to meet together to learn more about your exciting times."

"Sure," piped Elliot. "Ten minutes; we'll meet in front of the mission house."

"Yes, thank you," came Kasha's polite reply. She disappeared behind her father.

Rachel immediately stormed from the room, down the hallway and into her sleeping room. Elliot followed her from a distance. When he got to her doorway, she blasted him.

"You blabber!" she squeezed out.

"What?" he asked, startled.

"You! You blabbed all about our little finds didn't you?

To the lot of them . . . even the Mummy Mistress!"

"Goodness Agnes! They're archeologists for heaven's sake! Most of them are college professors, too. I thought they might have some helpful advice for us."

She had him backed into the corner.

"*She's* not a professor! She's nothing more than a summer intern at that dusty museum!"

"I didn't tell them everything. Dad and Dr. Ahmed don't know about the outbuilding. No reason to mention that until we've had a chance to check it out . . . which I intend to do shortly. Are you going with me?"

"Perhaps. Is she going?"

"Perhaps," Elliot echoed stubbornly.

Rachel jerked her waist pack from beside the bed and strapped it on.

"All right. Since you insist, I'll come. But I'm only doing this for you! I just hope Queen Tut brought more candy bars."

CHAPTER 8

Elliot retraced their steps from the night before, follow-ing a wide, circular path around the main excavations and past the man-made mounds of dug-out dirt where Rachel had unearthed the scarab. Kasha kept pace with him, acting interested in his constant jabber. In the five minutes it took to hike away from the mission, he managed to tell Kasha everything he and Rachel had done since leaving Cairo. Rachel, however, wanted no part of it. She walked several steps behind them, nursing her stinging sunburned scalp.

Soon the isolated outbuilding stood before them. It looked much the same as last night—plain, simple, easily overlooked. Elliot directed both of them to duck down where they were while he approached the straw-roofed mud house. After giving it a close inspection, he called out to them in a loud whisper.

"The lock is open! Someone's been here!"

Kasha turned to Rachel.

"Elliot told me you came here last night. It was locked then?"

Rachel shrugged and refused to look her companion in the eyes. "According to Mr. Junior Fossil, it was."

They watched as Elliot stepped lightly to the door and gave it a gentle push. The latch clicked open easily. He poked his head into the doorway, then his shoulders and satchel. Finally he stepped inside and disappeared completely.

Kasha settled closer to the ground. "He is very brave, your cousin."

"Pea-brained, I call it."

Elliot beckoned to them with a wave of his hand. The two of them advanced cautiously into the dim mudbrick structure which was lit only by the sunlight creeping through the cracks and crevices. Elliot had parked his shoulder bag in one corner. It bulged with all sorts of archeological doodads—a regular dirt-digger Santa-sack of goodies.

As near as Rachel could tell, the one-room hut was empty except for two large stone slabs resting on the floor like prehistoric cots. One seemed a bit tilted.

The cockeyed stone slab covered an area over three feet square. It appeared to be nearly ten inches thick, and Rachel had no doubt that the rectangular rock weighed much more than the three of them together could move.

"It's an entrance of some kind," Elliot said in a loud whisper.

"Most definitely," Kasha whispered back.

Rachel looked over each of her shoulders then blurted out, "Why are you whispering! There's no one here but us!"

Her cousin held a finger to his lips. "We don't know that for sure," came his quiet caution.

Kasha knelt beside the slab. Her long fingers traced one corner for any sign of a hand-hold. She bowed her head to the dirt, searching beneath the stone's edge. In the meantime, Elliot dug through his bag and handed Rachel a bundle of rope.

"I have seen stones such as this one lifted at excavation sites," Kasha confided. "When there are not enough workers to move a cover stone, a pulley system is set up so that one or two men may lift it."

"So," Elliot half joked, "we've got the rope. Now all we need is something to drape it over." His eyes began to scan the inner walls of the mudbrick building around them.

Kasha remained on the floor, her head pressed down next to one of the stone's sides. "I believe I found the opening. Yes . . . yes! This corner is loose!"

Rachel stepped only a little closer, not wanting to appear too interested in anything Kasha might find.

"There is a shaft," she went on, "a shaft not much smaller than the stone." She pressed her ear to the small black space, listened for a moment, then shook her head. "I cannot hear anything. I need . . ."

"Here," said Elliot before she finished her request. He tossed a pebble her way which she caught easily.

"How did you know what she wanted?" Rachel quizzed him.

"Old archeologist's trick . . . you drop the pebble down the hole and listen."

"No wonder all of you dirt-diggers are so boring. You

spend your lives dropping rocks down holes."

Kasha let the small stone slip from her hand. Eyes closed, ear to the stone slab, she lay silent. Suddenly her long black eyelashes fluttered.

"Dry . . . three to five meters . . . at least one other opening besides this one." Her announcement sounded like a riddle to be solved.

Elliot was tapping on the walls now.

"Man-made or natural?" he asked casually.

"Both, I would say."

Rachel decided to join the questioning.

"Is it animal, vegetable, or mineral?" Her two companions looked at her. "Is it bigger than a bread box? How many guesses do I have left?"

"I do not understand."

"Don't worry, Kasha," Elliot assured her. "There are times I don't understand either."

Rachel felt her face flush with anger and hurt. Instantly she went on the defensive.

"What's that supposed to mean? The two of you insist I accompany you here then talk in dirt-digger mumbo-jumbo and play a horribly rotten game of twenty questions!" In her disgust she threw the bundle of rope into the air. "Those clues were quite poor, I must tell you, but I shall have a guess anyway. I say a 'camel.' Camels are dry, three meters tall and they have at least two openings."

A broad grin spread across Kasha's face. It looked exactly like Elliot's frustrating grin, only this one had bigger teeth and softer lips. Problem was, Kasha wasn't grinning at Rachel. She was grinning at the ceiling.

"Bingo." Elliot's voice hung in the room.

"See?" crowed Rachel. "The answer *was* camel. I'm quite good at this game. Even with those ridiculous clues I figured it out."

Kasha and Elliot paid her no mind. Instead, both craned their necks upward toward the ceiling of the mud hut.

"That's odd," she suddenly realized. "The rope never came down."

"Like I said . . . Bingo," repeated Elliot.

Rachel stepped backwards and looked up. The looped bundle of rope hung above her head, suspended by a thick metal hook bolted to the hard ceiling.

"I think we just found our pulley," he smiled. "I'll give you three guesses why that big hook is positioned right above this big stone slab."

"Oh, no," Rachel shook her head. "Not another game. Anyway, you have to allow for twenty questions, not simply three."

Kasha hurriedly dusted her knees as she rose to help Elliot free the rope.

"I think our question about tomb robbers has now been answered," Kasha said to them both. "They have thought of everything, even the pulley hook in the ceiling to move the stone back and forth. The next question is . . . who?"

"Or why!" Elliot countered.

Two tugs on the rope and a loose end unfolded into Elliot's hands. The rope's middle length stayed above, draped over the big hook, leaving both ends dangling free. Kasha set to work forming a large slip knot at one end while Elliot struggled to find enough rope to tie around his waist with the other end. With Rachel's limited help, Kasha cinched the knot around the raised corner of the slab and stretched it taut. Elliot, meanwhile, took the rope in both hands, twisted it several times around his wrists, and braced himself against it. Slowly he pulled down on the rope. Full tension tightened on either side of the pulley hook as his weight attempted to move that of the cover stone. Athletic as he was, Elliot's lanky body couldn't force the slab. It would take all three of them, pulling together, to raise the stone just enough to uncover the shaft.

Kasha and Rachel found a place for their hands along the rope length. Elliot nodded out the count that would coordinate their movements. On the nod of three, they pulled with all of their might. The grinding sound of rock moving against rock spread inside the mud brick shack.

"Hang on! Keep pulling!" Elliot encouraged them.

Slowly the edge of the slab rose and inched to one, exposing the shaft beneath it which opened before them like a yawning, square mouth. Elliot released the rope. The slab dropped several inches to the hut's floor. Quickly as he could, he untied himself and scrambled to the hole.

"Goodness Agnes!" he whispered aloud. "There's a regular maze down here!"

Rachel was the last to reach the hole, having become entangled in the scratchy rope. Her eyes followed the narrow beam of Elliot's flashlight. Kasha's estimates were frighteningly accurate. Four meters below them lay a second mudbrick floor, dry as a bone, that had several corridors leading away from it. Someone had gone to a lot of time and trouble to construct this underground system, and hide it as well.

Elliot leaned back against the slab with a satisfied sigh. He adjusted his glasses and swiped at the sweat now forming on his forehead. The warming morning air combined with the effort involved in moving the stone had begun to heat the insides of the mudbrick building. The pink stripe in Rachel's scalp began to sting with sweat, making the cool draft of stale air rising up from the open shaft feel refreshing.

"Okay," Elliot said aloud, "we set a time limit, we go down and explore, then we climb out. I think thirty minutes should be long enough to find out what's going on. What do you think?"

Rachel started to answer but realized he was speaking to Kasha, who responded with a thoughtful nod.

"I suppose thirty minutes will be adequate," Rachel tacked on. She would not allow Sphinx Woman to get the best of her.

"We'll need a tie-off for the rope for both of us to go down," he went on, as if Rachel didn't exist.

"Or if you can lower me, I can search out more rope in the catacombs below," Kasha said, pushing in to plan the whole adventure—an adventure that should have been Rachel's. After all, it was her poked rear end that had led them here in the first place. She had found the gold beetle and the crusty thumb. All Elliot did was find this mud hut and bring a little rope.

"Here," Elliot said, digging deep into his shoulder

bag. Now he was talking to Rachel. He handed her a small plastic box the size of a telephone. "You'll need this if you're going to be the look-out."

"What's this for?"

"It's a walkie-talkie."

"I know *what* it is, Scarab Brain. What do you expect me to do with it?"

Kasha answered for him. "We will have the other one with us in the catacombs. When . . ."

"Wait a moment. I'm staying up here while the two of you go exploring down there? I don't think so." Rachel glanced around the dim room until her eyes fell on a metal loop jutting from the wall, about knee-high. Now *she* would take the reins of this expedition. "Tie off that blasted rope there, on that metal loop, and we'll all go down," she commanded. "I'll go first." The instant the words left her lips she wished they never had been spoken. Too late.

Elliot peeked over his shoulder and spied the loop. The corners of his mouth crinkled slightly in approval.

"Not a bad idea."

"Tie me off, then." Rachel got on her stomach and carefully scooted backwards until her feet hung over the shaft's sharp edge. Her cousin made a small stir-rup at one end of the rope then handed it to her. He cinched the other around his own arms.

"If we tie off, you'll be six feet short at the bottom. Not good. I'll lower you. Then Kasha and I can anchor the rope to the wall loop for us and drop the last six feet if we need to." He hesitated. "You know what you're doing?"

"Of course!" she bluffed loudly. "I've explored my share of cattle combs! Get on with it!"

One foot in the stirrup loop, she moved farther into the hole with Elliot guiding her.

"That's it . . . back down slowly . . . a little farther . . ."

Rachel felt her stomach dragging down the lip of the shaft until only her elbows and head rested above ground. Her hands held the rope so tightly they trembled.

"You've got the easy part, you know," Elliot assured her. "Kasha and I will have to tie off up here and jump-kick our way down like mountain climbers."

"Stop blabbering and hold that rope!" she retorted.

"Now, push off lightly with your feet against the inner wall, and I'll let you down a foot or so."

Against her better judgment, Rachel did as he asked. He dropped her the short distance as promised, but the resulting jolt made her heart leap in her chest.

"Sorry," he quickly blurted. "I just wish we had more rope."

The rope swayed gently, moving back and forth between the vertical walls of the shaft. It wasn't a terribly wide hole; in fact, Rachel thought she could almost reach both sides at the same time by simply stretching out her arms.

"Try not to move," Elliot instructed her. "The more you move, the harder you are to hold."

"Lovely. You don't know how good that makes me feel," Rachel snapped. Suddenly the rope seemed short indeed.

"How much farther to the bottom?" Elliot grunted.

Rachel tried to look down but, in the process, knocked the clumsy dig hat from her head.

"Blast! I haven't the foggiest! I'm not a bat, you know . . . I can't see in the dark!" She wished it were Kasha's cat-like eyes and not her own hanging in this hole. "And I've dropped that stupid hat of yours! I told you it wouldn't fit!"

Without warning the rope slipped, dropping Rachel nearly a meter before stopping her with a nasty jerk. She felt a rope burn forming on her hands.

"All right!" she cried. "That is it. Get me out of here this instant!" She pulled as hard as she could against the rope with hopes of climbing out hand-over-hand.

"Don't pull!" wailed Elliot.

The rope shuddered. The sound of scuffling feet told Rachel that Kasha had joined Elliot at the other end of the rope, straining furiously to keep it steady. Somehow, with Rachel dangling at one end and her companions pulling against her weight on the other, the rope began to twist. She felt its scratchy cords squeeze her forearm and its rough twine burn against her palms. Slowly, she swung side to side like the pendulum of some old clock. With each pass the rope scraped hard against the sharp edge of the shaft opening. After several passes the rope untwisted, twirling Rachel in small, tight circles.

As she spun around and around, her stomach moved into her throat and her head grew light and woozy. Tiny jolts vibrating down the knotted rope jiggled her foot loose from its slip-knot stirrup. Both feet now swayed free in the cool updraft of stale air.

Only Rachel's cramping arms, clinging to the rope, kept her from the uncertain fate awaiting her at the shaft's bottom. She clenched her fingers hard around the rope, yanked with all her strength and swung her heels upwards to gain a better hold. The strain of her panic, however, exhausted the now frayed rope.

The last things she saw were the soles Elliot's shoes braced against the shaft edge and the terrified look on Kasha's bronzed face.

"Rachel!"

With one final jolt, the last strand of rope gave out. *Snap!*

CHAPTER 9

Rachel awoke to the glare of a flashlight scanning her face. A dull pain throbbed through her back and into her neck.

"Rachel! Rachel!" Elliot's distant voice echoed around her.

She found herself lying flat on her back with her waist pack and Elliot's borrowed hat beside her. As she drew a breath to answer a sharper, more urgent pain pressed from her shoulder. She groaned softly.

"Rachel!"

"Are you all right?"

Now two voices called down to her. Slowly, she focused her eyes. Then she remembered—the mud hut, the slab, Queen Tut, the rope and . . .

"Can you stand?" Kasha asked from above. She sounded concerned.

"Move that blasted flashlight out of my face," she moaned. "It's bad enough that I'm dying . . . you needn't blind me as well!"

"Yes! She's okay!" Elliot cried.

She could barely make out Elliot's outline and his toothy grin.

Rachel struggled to a sitting position despite her backache. Elliot's face peered down at her.

"Is anything broken?"

"Of course something's broken. The rope!" Rachel howled back. "Fix it and get me out of here!"

"Uhh, we're working on that." She heard the two mumbling to one another. At last Elliot spoke up. "We need a new rope, Rachel. Dad has one at the excavation site. It'll take me fifteen minutes to get it. Just hang tight and I'll be right back." He knelt at the top of the shaft. "Here, take these." A small cloth bag sailed down the opening and landed with a thunk beside her feet. He pulled his hat from his head and leaned as far into the shaft as possible. "I'm not leaving until I'm sure you're all right."

Slowly Rachel stood up to encourage Elliot's departure.

"You've got fourteen minutes left on that flashy watch of yours. I'm waiting."

The door of the hut swung open, then closed with a clunk. He was gone.

"Perhaps you should walk a little. You will feel better." Rachel squinted up at Kasha with one eye.

"Walk? In case you haven't noticed, I'm at the bottom of a hole!"

"Yes. I know how you feel."

"And?" Rachel said in her matter-of-fact tone.

"I was once trapped in a tomb near the Valley of the Kings. Unfortunately, my directions became confused. It took my father nearly two days to find me."

"Two days?"

Kasha nodded and chuckled at the memory.

"What did you eat?" wondered Rachel.

"Nothing . . . until I was rescued. Then I ate my words—only one week before I had told everyone I could find my way through any tomb maze that existed."

Rachel gave her sore shoulder a brief massage. "I imagine you felt quite foolish."

"Yes. I still do. Please . . . do not tell Elliot. I do not wish him to think of me as foolish."

"Oh, I wouldn't worry if I were you. He's had his share of rash moments." She couldn't think of one that instant but felt certain he had a past filled with foolishness. Somewhere.

"Elliot? Foolish?"

"Indeed!" Rachel relished the moment. "I shall tell you all about it sometime."

"I would like that." Kasha smiled.

Rachel caught herself smiling back but quickly erased it.

"So . . . how far down the tunnel can you see?" Kasha inquired.

Rachel turned away from the shaft. "Not far. I suppose I could have a look while I'm down here."

"I believe Elliot slipped his flashlight into the bag he dropped for you. Perhaps it would be helpful?"

The flashlight lay just inside the mouth of the bag. Rachel switched it on and put Elliot's hat back on her head to add to the adventurous mood. To her surprise, three tunnels led away from the shaft landing. Cautiously she inched into one of them.

"There are three hallways, actually." One by one she directed the flashlight down the catacomb corridors. "Head-chopper height I should say—if I don't duck a bit I shall bonk Elliot's extra hat."

"I can barely hear you. Try using the walkie-talkie."

Rachel rummaged through the bag and found the walkie-talkie at the bottom beneath a large ball of twine, a second flashlight, some matches, and other assorted dirt-digger items. She took the walkie-talkie from the bag and clicked the on button. The hand-held unit crackled to. Kasha's voice broke through the static for a moment.

"Can you hear me, Rachel?"

She pressed the talk button and held it down to reply. "Yes. I can see three separate cattle combs. Two of them seem to go on for quite some distance." She shuffled into the entrance of the opening to her right, hauling the bag with her. Two meters, three meters . . . suddenly a tall, narrow figure stood in her path. She gasped and dropped the walkie-talkie—on her foot.

"What is happening?" chirped the fallen walkie-talkie.

Rachel drew her flashlight like a six-shooter and shone it straight into the eyes of the thing blocking her. A pair of hieroglyphs stared back. A sigh of relief escaped from her throat.

Rachel knelt and picked up the speaker. "Nothing. I've stumbled onto one of those boring rock obelisks your father is so keen on. It's littered with Egyptian carvings—birds, symbols, pots, and all that rot."

"Obelisk? I do not understand. What are obelisks doing here at Tell ed-Daba?"

Rachel waltzed around the stone pillar before she answered. "You're asking me? I thought you were the obelisk expert!"

"My father, perhaps. But, like you, I am not 'keen' on them. I prefer the mummies."

Rachel forged on into the half-darkness of the catacomb. Just a short distance ahead the tunnel took a bend to the left. Five meters later it twisted right, then jogged left again. At each turn, Rachel noticed various carvings on pillars used to shore up the catacomb walls. Hieroglyphs. Kasha radioed her at almost every step.

"How far have you gone?" Kasha asked. "Have you come to the end of the tunnel?"

"This isn't a football match! I can't keep giving you play-by-play!" Rachel retorted, walkie-talkie in hand. She kept her 'talk' button pressed for an extra moment so Kasha couldn't contact her. Then she thought better of it and decided to give a real answer. "Actually, I see no sign of it ending. I've passed by several twists and turns . . ." An ear-piercing squeal blared from the tiny speaker in Rachel's hand. She tapped it, softly at first, then hard, with her fist. Nothing happened. "What is wrong with this thing? How do I shut it up?" She released her button to hear Kasha's reply.

"There is a knob on the side. Turn it down until the noise is gone."

Rachel tried Kasha's suggestion and, to no surprise, it worked just as she said it would.

"You should turn back now. Elliot will return soon. Go no farther into the catacomb or you may be lost."

Rachel only half-listened to her, for she had come to a room adjacent to the catacomb corridor. The flashlight beam searched its walls and fell upon a number of interesting items. The longer she looked, the more interested she became.

"Amazing!" she heard herself gasp. Quickly she pulled the walkie-talkie to her mouth and pressed the button. "Amazing!" she repeated for Kasha's benefit. "It almost looks like the museum in Cairo down here."

The excited voice at the other end of the radio blurted something Rachel couldn't understand. So she waited for Kasha to repeat it, which she did a moment later.

"Can you hear me? I said 'what have you found that is like the Museum?'"

"Everything. All of it," she replied, her eyes scanning the room from behind the flashlight's limited path. "Pots, little statues of men marching . . ." She turned to face another wall. "Big stone tablets with Egyptian writing, a spear of some sort . . . some jewelry . . . a gold box . . . hello, what's this?" She laid the walkie-talkie and flashlight aside and used both hands to lift a life-sized mummy mask lying on a stone ledge along the wall. All the while Kasha's voice buzzed in the speaker.

"Rachel! Rachel!"

"So . . . someone's set up his own little Egyptian museum here in this hole in the middle of nowhere," Rachel mumbled aloud. Elliot's hunch must be correct: modern-day tomb robbers were using this ancient set of catacombs—originally carved out by the slaves of an early Pharaoh—to stash goods stolen from dozens of dig sites across northern Egypt. And what a stash! "Dung beetles, indeed!" she mumbled again. These treasures made the little gold bug they found yesterday seem like a good-for-nothing bug just waiting to be squished.

"Rachel!" Kasha's tone sounded urgent.

"Yes, yes, yes! I'm coming!" Rachel wasn't certain if she had pressed the 'talk' button or not. Frankly, she didn't care, as interested as she was in the things around her.

"Elliot has returned," bleeped the walkie-talkie. "He has your uncle's rope. Come to the opening."

Rachel thought she heard a rope slap against the hard mudbrick floor somewhere in the dimness. As she gathered the walkie-talkie and Elliot's bag, she thought she heard something else. A faint, almost unnatural squeaking sound that seemed to come from a pile of treasures near the floor.

"Mice," she told herself. "It must be mice that have found their way in. We found *our* way in, after all. Surely some dumb mouse could do the same."

"Rachel . . ." This time the voice at the other end of the radio was Elliot's. "We're waiting."

She lifted the walkie-talkie to her mouth and squeezed the button extra hard.

"Waiting? Oh, really. What do you think *I've* been doing . . . playing hopscotch? Where have you been? You're late." She had no watch, of course, but hoped Elliot had used up more than the agreed fifteen minutes.

"I've been gone less than five minutes, Rachel. Just

come back and we'll pull you out."

As she left the catacomb room the bag in her hand
caught on a sharp stone statue, ripping a hole in the
side of the bag. Elliot's precious dig stuff tumbled out
onto the floor.

"Rot!" Hastily Rachel gathered the items into a pile.
She could leave them—and endure at least one
'Goodness Agnes!' from Elliot—or she could figure a
way to haul them without the bag. Suddenly, a narrow
strip of cloth draped over the stone statue gave her an
idea. She took the cloth strip from the statue, wrapped
it around the torn bag, and tied it all together like a
knapsack.

Crossing back into the tunnel a second time, Rachel
found herself faced with a choice: left . . . or right?

"Right. I believe it is right," she tried to convince herself. "On second thought, I'm certain it is left. Yes,
that's it. Left." A long moment passed as she stood in
front of the treasure room entrance. Then the unearthly squeaking sound returned. The sound—and the
darkness—prompted her to swallow all pride and press
the 'talk' button.

"Uhhh . . . I seem to have misplaced something."

"What?" Elliot asked.

"The shaft." The quiver of mild panic she felt must
have come through in her voice. Kasha answered her
calmly.

"You are quite near the opening, I am sure. Just tell
me where you are now."

What good will that do? she thought. *Kasha has no
idea where I am.*

"I'm facing the room filled with artifacts. But . . ."

"Take the tunnel to your right," buzzed the walkie-talkie. "Soon it will curve . . . follow it until you reach another fork in the catacomb." Rachel headed right, just as the radio squawked again. "When you pass the fork, remain to your left. You should notice more light shining into the catacomb. Walk toward the faint light. The shaft is there on the left."

Rachel followed the invisible map Kasha drew for her. Some of the territory looked vaguely familiar. Much of it did not. She feared the worst would happen: that she would become lost in the maze of tomb-like passageways, grow faint, and starve to death while Elliot and Kasha sat meters away munching on candy bars. Within sixty seconds, however, she found herself standing beneath the opening, staring up at Kasha's cat eyes and Elliot's moth-eaten hat.

"How did you get me here?" she exclaimed, looking up through the narrow shaft. "How did you know *how* to get me here?"

Kasha held up a small piece of paper with lines and arrows. "A map. I recorded your steps as you explored the tomb catacombs."

"Jolly good idea, that."

"Just grab the rope . . . and hurry." Elliot seemed unusually anxious.

"Here . . . take your rotten bag up first. Nearly broke my toe," she mumbled loudly. She tied the bag onto the rope's end. Elliot hauled it up with quick, short jerks, removed the bag, looped a slip knot into the scratchy cord then again dropped the rope. Rachel stepped into the slip-knot stirrup and hugged the rope as the other two hoisted her to the surface. The moment her shoulders cleared the opening Elliot pulled her to safety.

Before she could speak to blame him for the rope mishap, he pressed one hand over her lips and placed a finger to his own, then whispered.

"Shhhhh! I thought I heard voices." He was staring into the shaft. "Down there."

The three remained motionless, listening. Soon Kasha broke their silence.

"I hear nothing."

"Neither do I," Rachel chimed in. "There's probably some small rodent living in that filthy hat of yours. And should you ever drop me down a hole again, you shall be hearing more than rodent voices!"

Without delay, he coiled the rope into a tight bundle and crammed it into the cloth bag. He didn't quiz her on what she found in the tomb; in fact, it was obvious that Kasha had not let Elliot in on their secret little room down below. Either that, or he was in an incredible hurry.

Rachel waited on the ground until he offered her assistance, then she rose slowly with great drama. And a faked limp.

"Internal injuries. Head injury. Concussion. Amoeba," she stated flatly. "I do believe that fall has caused them all."

"Amoeba?" questioned Elliot. "I think you mean 'amnesia.'"

"See there? I've already lost part of my memory!"

"We can argue later. Right now I think we should get out of here."

Kasha took a cautious peek outside the door.

"We are alone. I can hear faint voices coming from the excavation site, however. Perhaps that is what you heard."

"Maybe." Elliot shrugged. He didn't seem convinced. "Let's go."

"What about the stone slab?" Kasha said.

"Let's get Rachel back to the dig first. Hopefully, the tomb robbers . . . assuming there really *are* tomb robbers . . . won't return until dark. We'll come back later, check out the tomb, and cover the shaft."

They slipped from the mudbrick building, closed the door behind them, and set out for the mission house. Rachel made certain she lagged behind, nursing her injuries while Elliot shouldered all of the equipment. Suddenly he stopped dead in his tracks.

"I thought you were in a hurry!" Rachel scolded.

Slowly, he raised the cloth bag to eye level.

"Goodness Agnes! Where did you find this?"

CHAPTER 10

Rachel hobbled up behind him, purposely taking her own sweet time.

"Don't tell me you've suffered a case of amoeba as well!" she retorted.

"Amnesia," he corrected her.

"Whatever. In case you have forgotten, that happens to be the bag you threw down the hole . . . after my unfortunate fall. I'm still not certain I'll survive, by the way. Had I been a meter higher my liver might have . . ."

Kasha had now joined Elliot in examining the bag.

"What do you think?" he asked Kasha. "Hyksos period?"

She nodded. "Possibly. The designs, and the weave in the cloth almost look Semitic."

"Are you listening to me?" Rachel plunged on. "Just what is it you find so fascinating about that old bag?" She hobbled her way to where they stood, then cringed a bit at the sight of the careless rip running along one side. "All right, then. I plead guilty. I did manage to tear a tiny hole in the old thing . . . but it was dark. I didn't see that stupid statue."

Elliot turned toward her slowly and adjusted his glasses. His green eyes flashed into her own.

"Statue? What statue?"

"Oh, just some old thing I saw in the tomb back there. Nothing, really. Just a statue . . . and not a very good one at that. It had a body like a man, but the head looked like a bird. The bag caught on the beak of the ugly thing . . ."

Elliot spun to face Kasha, his face filled with questions.

"I think there are several artifacts in the catacombs," she said. "Perhaps your theory of tomb robbers is correct."

"Are there any other pieces of cloth like this one?" Elliot grilled her. He gently unwrapped the narrow strip of fabric from around the bag, the strip Rachel had borrowed from the bird statue, and held it out to her. It was the cloth, not the bag, they were interested in.

"I don't know. There were lots of things in the room and . . ."

"Room?" he broke in.

"Kasha and I did a little snooping while you chased after rope. I found a tomb room . . ." She grinned a mischievous grin. "I like the sound of that . . . 'tomb room' . . . don't you?" For once, she had information he didn't, and she planned to make the most of it. "Actually, I prefer to call it a 'treasure room.'"

"Goodness Agnes! Why didn't you say so earlier?"

"Because I have a fatal back injury. And because you were in such a dash to get out of that mud hut."

Elliot heaved a sigh of frustration, trying to be patient.

"I hurried you because I heard something—or some-one—down in that underground tomb." He rubbed his forehead a moment. "Okay. We'll go back to the mission house and start from the beginning . . . what you saw, where you saw it . . ."

He gathered the bag, slung it over his shoulders, and led them toward the mission house. Kasha stayed behind to walk with Rachel. "Is there anything else you remember seeing in the tomb?"

"I'm not certain. There are lots of things in that room. But it was quite dark. And falling down the shaft didn't help my concentration any."

"Mmmmm." Kasha hesitated before she went on. "I think you should know," she confided, "Elliot was quite concerned about you and your fall into the tomb entrance."

"Really?" she said dryly. "Concerned about that hat of his I borrowed, perhaps."

"No. About you. He told me it should have been him instead down in the shaft."

"He's got that right. It *should* have been him," she bluffed. Kasha's shocked looked forced Rachel to give a more honest answer. She hung her head a little. "Actually, I'm not surprised he said that. And I have no doubt he meant every word. That's just how Elliot is . . ." She gave Kasha a sly smirk. "Just one of those foolish faults of his I hinted at earlier."

Kasha looked at the ground, smiling to herself.

"Did I just say something good about that pea-brain?" Rachel quickly countered. "Because if I did, it was a mistake. He is my cousin . . . and one can't choose

one's relatives, you know. So I am stuck with him."
They walked a few steps further. Rachel gave up the
fake limp so Kasha wouldn't have to walk so slowly.

"Actually," she continued, "you and he are quite
alike. Not the pea-brain part, of course, but . . . well . . .
if Elliot had a sister, I believe she would be a great deal
like you. You wouldn't have to look like him, you realize.
You could look like Uncle Mason . . . or like Elliot's
mother, perhaps."

"What does his mother look like?"

"She's gone now, and I don't really remember her too
well. I *do* recall that she was quite lovely. And she got on
well with my mother, so she must have been a saint."

"If I were Elliot's sister that would make the two of us
cousins, would it not?" A kind smile rose on Kasha's
face.

"Yes, I suppose it would."

They walked in silence, slowly catching up to Elliot
as they neared the Austrian mission buildings. Finally
Rachel had to get an answer to a question that burned
in her mind. "Why didn't you tell Elliot all about the
tomb discoveries earlier?"

"Well, the discoveries belong to you. I believe you
should be the one to tell about them. I guess it is what
archeologists call 'professional courtesy.'"

Rachel wasn't much on courtesy. But she thought
she understood.

"Besides," Kasha added, "we are almost cousins,
right?"

Elliot reached the mission house well before them.
By the time they arrived he had dumped the equip-

ment bag and set up shop in a corner work area. A magnifying glass the size of an orange rested in one hand. The narrow strip of cloth from the tomb lay on the worktable before him.

"Kasha," he said, peering through the big glass eyepiece, "take a look at this."

She hurried to his side. Rachel could almost see her transformation from 'teenaged Queen Tut' to 'deepthinking archeologist' as she pondered the colored cloth strip.

"It looks to be wool," she offered.

"And I'm convinced the designs are Semitic." Elliot nodded to confirm his own thoughts. "See the repeating zig-zag pattern?"

"Mmmmm." The Egyptian girl leaned closer to the magnifying glass.

"Sea midgets?" Rachel broke in. "What are you talking about? I didn't see any small ocean animals in that tomb—I'm certain of that."

"Not sea midgets," Elliot corrected her. "Semitic. This strip of cloth looks like a waist band of some kind . . . probably made by ancient people living east of Egypt, like the Israelites or the Canaanites."

Kasha nodded, so Rachel nodded, too.

"Oh, yes, of course. The Camel-lights. Weren't they somehow related to the Donkey-lights?" Rachel went on. She wasn't sure she had the names quite right, but they sounded impressive.

Elliot adjusted his hat.

"Somehow I don't think so," he mumbled from behind a faint grin.

"There definitely is hand stitching along the edges," observed Kasha. "It must have been used as a wrap-around, to tie back clothing, or curtains."

"Or . . ." Elliot's eyes narrowed behind his glasses. "Let me take another look at that cloth." He borrowed the magnifying glass from Kasha and, starting at one end, inched his way down the length of the strip. "It's over three feet long, it has the proper pattern designs, the colors are right . . ." He held the cloth straight out from his nose where it dangled like a wooly snake striped with colors of blue, red, and black. A small, red-dish tassel hung from the bottom end. "Rachel . . ." he quizzed, "what does this look like to you?"

"An absolutely horrid necktie."

"No, seriously."

She studied the cloth strip, knowing full well that Mr. and Miss Junior Archeologist were waiting for her answer. Not wanting to disappoint Kasha, she tried her best to give an honest one.

"Well, actually . . . it looks like the belt to Uncle Mason's old bathrobe—the one that always hangs in the guest bath."

"Exactly." Elliot held the strip of cloth to his waist. The tassel hung down the side. "It's a little long for me, but it would probably fit a person, say, sixteen or seventeen years old, don't you think?"

Kasha sat, her eyes wide with interest. She looked as if an idea had struck her. Then she spoke.

"Are you familiar with the excavations here at Tell ed-Daba—those thought by some to be the tomb of Joseph the Israelite?"

"Yep. But not half as familiar as you are. Can you tell us more about them?"

"There are several digs on the other side of the Tell," she began. "One appears to be the foundation of a small palace. Near it is a single, exposed tomb of mud-brick. The damaged statue of a foreigner, a Semite, was found there. It is the only artifact from the burial chamber. All others, including the mummy laid to rest there, must have been removed long ago." Kasha paused, then asked in a hushed tone: "Do you believe the robe of the young Joseph is hidden in the tomb shaft Rachel discovered today?"

"I asked him the same question," Rachel butted in proudly.

"Could be," Elliot said with his winning grin. "There's only one way to find out . . . go back and look for it."

Rachel found a comfortable spot to lounge, slipped Elliot's borrowed hat from her head, and dusted the front of her shirt. "Well, I hope the two of you have a jolly good time romping around on your tomb tour. Should you need me, I shall be right here—feet up and candy bars in hand. My body has had enough archeological adventure for one lifetime, thank you."

Obviously, Elliot wasn't listening.

"I wonder if we'll have enough light with only our flashlights."

Rachel jumped in, making certain Elliot understood her plans. "Keep in mind, you'll only be needing two flashlights. I shan't be going down that hole again."

"I'll borrow a couple of hand torches from the Austrians. From the sounds of it, there may be a lot of ground to cover down in that old tomb-turned-hideout. He adjusted his hat and glasses, and crossed his arms. Then he gazed through his wire-rimmed glasses at Rachel. "We need you down there. You're the only one who knows what's in that 'treasure room' of yours."

"No, no, no. I have no plans to crack my spine into little pieces twice in one day."

"Promise me you'll think about it while I get the torches. That's all I ask." He was off.

She had little time to think for he returned in a flash, carrying something under his arm.

"I ran into Dr. Mueller," Elliot explained. "The torches are stored here at the mission house, so he gave me a couple." He drew three sticks from beneath his arm.

"What are those?" Rachel wondered.

Elliot held up the meter-long sticks.

"Hand torches," he answered. "To use in the tomb."

She studied them for a moment. The long sticks resembled giant black Q-tips, with wooden handles. "Oh, you won't be needing those. You can just use the ones that are already in the tomb."

Elliot's jaw dropped wide open. "What?"

"There must be a dozen of them, down in the cattle combs."

Kasha and he exchanged a long, knowing glance.

"What! What did I say?" defended Rachel.

"Where did you see them?" Elliot sputtered out.

"I told you, in the cattle combs. Most were stacked up in one of the tunnels. Although a few hung on the walls. They weren't lit, mind you. But they smelled of kerosene."

Elliot grasped her shoulders between his hands and pressed her into a seat. "Do something for me, will you? Tell me what in the world you saw down there today! Everything!"

"If you insist!" She turned to address Kasha. "He's such a picky one, you know." Rachel then proceeded to tell them all she remembered—the tunnel mazes, the hieroglyphs, the torches, the statues, the 'treasure room'—she even told of the gold mummy mask.

"And there was this . . . this high-pitched squeaking sound. I only heard it once or twice, but it certainly sounded creepy. I imagine it was mice roaming about in all that junk." She nodded her head in thought. "That's all of it, then."

Her cousin slumped back into his chair, sorry he couldn't start the return trip immediately. He checked his space-age watch.

"I promised Dad we would help at the excavation after lunch," he addressed Rachel. "When we finish we'll meet here before we go back to the tomb."

"I also can help at the dig," Kasha offered.

Rachel didn't waver.

"As I told you before, I shall be doing neither. I shall be right here, nursing my ruptured gall bladder."

Elliot spoke to her in a firm yet patient way, the same way Uncle Mason spoke to his students at the museum.

"From what you've told us, there is no doubt that tomb robbers have made off with dozens, maybe hundreds of ancient Egyptian treasures. We're the only ones able to save those treasures, or—to use your words—'to save the past for our future.'"

"I suppose I *did* say that, didn't I?"

Elliot continued his pep talk. "It will take all of us. I can't promise it will be easy. I can't promise it will be safe. But I *can* promise an adventure. And that's why we're all here, isn't it?"

Kasha nodded a supportive 'yes.'

Rachel, however, simply wanted to pop him one on the head.

CHAPTER 11

"For the record," Rachel harped, "I do not support this plan to go back down into that hole. It is dark, it is creepy, and it is four meters deep—deeper if you go down head first."

"You're right," came Elliot's shocking reply. Then he hit her with a dose of his frustrating logic. "But . . . going back down for those artifacts is the right thing to do."

"Did I mention there were mice?" she added.

"Think of it this way . . . if there are mice, there must not be snakes."

She held her peace. As usual, Elliot won the argument before it began. So she changed the subject. "This scratchy rope is beginning to rub blisters on my shoulder."

"We've almost reached the outbuilding, Rachel," he replied flatly. He didn't offer to carry it for her. Apparently he thought the satchel, torches, and artifact bag across his shoulders were load enough.

"Blisters can become infected," she rattled on. "And

once infection sets in, it's just a matter of time until the worst."

"Here, I will help you." Kasha shifted her own shoulder bag to one side to make room for Rachel's rope.

Elliot shook his head in patient dismay. Then he let out a grin. "I notice you've lost your limp this afternoon."

"And lucky for you I have!" Rachel quickly countered. "You should feel fortunate that my body has such wonderful natural healing powers."

"Probably from all of those candy bars."

Rachel reflexively squeezed at the small travel pack around her waist, feeling for the extra rectangles of chocolate and almonds Kasha had brought them from Cairo. They were still there.

"I really am sorry about the rope this morning," Elliot said. "I thought sending you down first was the safest thing to do."

"Apology accepted. Although that doesn't mean I'll forget it happened." Rachel dabbed at the sweat under the brim of her dig hat. It would feel good to get out of the brutal sun—even if it meant returning to the tomb. She knew her sunburned scalp would appreciate it.

Soon they reached the outbuilding, just as Elliot promised. It appeared exactly as they had left it, except for its long shadow in the late-afternoon sun. The door remained unlocked, the obelisk leaned against the outer wall. Inside, the stone slab still lay to one side. An invisible whisper of cool air rose from the open tomb shaft.

Elliot borrowed the rope from Kasha's shoulder and

formed a large lasso knot in one end.

"Be right back," he promised. He stepped out into the late-day sunlight for a moment. Soon he returned with the large bundle of rope still in his hands. One end trailed behind him, disappearing beneath the mud-hut door. "I've tied off to the helpful obelisk leaned against the outer wall," he announced. "That should hold all of us—at the same time, if necessary."

Kasha squatted to look down the shaft then glanced up at the ceiling hook.

"We have enough rope to lift out artifacts using the pulley hook."

"Right. Now, do we have everything?"

Kasha unzipped the satchel and announced its contents. "Twine, matches, flashlights, walkie-talkies, camera . . ."

"Candy bars?" Rachel broke in.

"I thought you brought your own candy bars," Elliot reminded her.

"I may have packed one, or possibly two at the most," she lied. "But one can never have enough. What if we become stranded? For two days?" She cast a knowing glance at Kasha. "Without candy bars, how would we survive?"

"By eating these." He pulled a bag of carrots from the shoulder bag.

"Lovely. What do you intend to do with those—start a rabbit farm?"

Quickly Kasha dug several chocolate bars from her bag. "We are in luck." She smiled at Rachel. "A two-day supply."

Elliot peeked through a narrow crack in the mudhut door. After adjusting his glasses, he spoke.

"We're losing daylight. We'd better get going if we plan to finish before dark." Tugging at the rope to test its strength, he turned his back to the shaft then walked backwards with the rope wrapped tightly around his wrists. "I'll go first," he announced to Rachel. He squirmed down to his stomach, slipped beyond the shaft ledge, and scrambled safely down the scratchy rope in less than ten seconds. Only the glint of light reflecting off his eyeglasses was visible from the hole as he called up: "Next!"

"Please, you go," Kasha suggested. "I will be last."

Rachel liked the idea of being in the middle. That way, if something went wrong on either end, she had someone to blame.

Her trip down the rope went much easier this time around. Like Elliot, she climbed down hand-over-hand without a problem. Moments later, Kasha's long form and wavy hair blocked what little light filtered down the shaft. The thud of her feet against the mudbrick floor signaled that all three were safely down.

Elliot's flashlight clicked on and he rummaged through his satchel.

"The plan is stick together," he instructed them. "But if we happen to get separated, or if we lose our way, we'll need to find our way back here." He handed each of them a piece of twine. Each string led to a large roll of twine that sat on a metal rod built into a frame. "Tie this twine around your waist. I'll prop the frame behind this obelisk . . . " he said, motioning to the stone pillar that had surprised Rachel earlier, ". . . so the twine can spin. Just like kite string." Kasha had already tied her kite string—clearly she had done this before. "It rolls out as we walk," explained Elliot.

"Like dropping bread crumbs?" Rachel thought out-loud. "To find our way home."

"Right."

"I rather like this idea," she said, cheerily slipping the twine around her middle. "It's quite clever. Must be a trick you dirt-diggers borrowed from someone else."

Elliot ignored her, tied his string, and cinched up his satchel bag. "We can collect any small artifacts in here." He patted the shoulder bag. "Like mummies' thumbs," he added, with a tip of his hat.

"What *is* all this business about mummy append-ages?" Rachel burst out. "And why would anyone—even lowly tomb robbers—stuff two-zillion-year-old thumbs into gold beetle statues. Were they saving them for a late-night snack or something?"

Kasha and Elliot exchanged serious glances. Her cousin spoke first.

"Not exactly. But you're in the ballpark."

"What is that supposed to mean?"

"I've already promised not to give her any more dis-gusting information. So I guess it's your turn." Elliot nodded to Kasha, who shrugged her shoulders the same way Elliot did before delivering bad news.

"Sometimes, ancient objects . . . like tomb wrappings or mummy parts . . . are ground into powders and sold."

"What on earth for?"

"Money," Elliot jumped in.

"I figured that out, Mummy Meister. I mean for what purpose?"

"Health and beauty products," said Kasha.

Rachel frowned, prompting Elliot to give his answer.

"People eat them. They think eating mummies will make them live longer. Happy now?"

"I believe I shall be sick." Rachel leaned against the catacomb wall.

"It is best not to dwell on these thoughts," Kasha advised her. "Let us be going."

Elliot's string pulled taut behind him as he led them deeper into the catacomb tunnel. Rachel followed behind the blurry ray of his flashlight with Kasha at her rear. She still felt a bit queasy.

"This has got to be an old tomb," he observed.

"I agree."

Kasha shined her flashlight on the nearest stone pillar which formed part of a catacomb entrance, and traced the designs with her finger.

"These hieroglyphs are etched into original stone and mudbrick. This was a tomb. From my experience, it probably was the tomb of a lower-ranking family, built to hold a number of mummies. Certainly it is not made for a pharaoh."

"But the layout is classic—a long passageway, a handful of dead-end catacombs fashioned to confuse ancient tomb robbers—I'm just surprised to find it here at Tell ed-Daba."

"Please!" Rachel pleaded. "Don't say 'dead.' It only reminds me of the disgusting things these thieves are doing with mummy parts." She pressed her waist pack against her churning stomach. Her stash of candy bars pressed back, calming her.

"The place sure has come in handy for modern-day tomb robbers, though." Elliot turned to Rachel. "So . . . can you lead us from here to this 'treasure room' of yours?"

She motioned him forward.

"Just move through the twists and turns and stay to your right."

Elliot did as she told him, which pleased her greatly. It also tempted her to lead him on some wild goose chase through the tunnels as he obeyed her every command. Problem was, she would get them all lost and end up having to share candy bars. It would almost be worth it. Almost.

They moved along slowly, their hands brushing the old walls at each bend. Columns of Egyptian symbols were etched into pillars along their path, containing long-forgotten messages of people and times gone by. The coolness of the underground air tickled Rachel's arms and legs. The darkening tunnel sent a chill or two up her spine.

Several dead-end catacombs later Rachel spotted a familiar set of wall hieroglyphs. "There! I do believe that's it just ahead, to the right."

Kasha shone her flashlight down the carved-out cata-comb. Eerie shadows bounced and shifted in its beam.

"Okay. Let's break out the torches," Elliot said, kneel-ing to unload the three giant, black Q-tips from under his arm. Rachel knelt with him, making certain her string was still anchored to the tomb entrance by reaching behind her back and giving the lifeline a gentle tug. Elliot brought out a box of matches and struck the first one to life. It flared then snuffed itself out. A second match quivered slightly beneath their gaze.

"Mmmmm. That's odd." In the fragile glow of matchlight Rachel saw a furrow appear in Elliot's brow. Again the flame whipped back and forth as if blown like a candle on a birthday cake. Instantly he smothered the match then sat stone-still in the surrounding darkness.

"Excuse me," Rachel said in the most irritating British accent she could muster. "As I recall, your mission was to light these stupid Q-tips, not to squat in this hole to play with matches."

His voice came as a damp, cool whisper from the dark. "There's another entrance to this tomb . . . besides the one we entered. And it's open. That's why the matches keep flickering; there's a draft moving through here."

Kasha squeezed in tighter between Rachel and Elliot. "Did you hear something?" she whispered.

"Not yet."

"This isn't funny, Elliot Conner. I've already fallen down this hole once today. I'm in no mood for these 'Looney Tomb' games of yours." Rachel shifted her weight from one knee to the other. "You're the one who insisted we take on this 'Save the Artifacts' campaign. Now, are we lighting the Q-tips or not?"

A long silence followed. Then a third match struck to life. Behind its glow lay a concerned face sporting wire-rimmed glasses. "Watch your step. Be careful. Don't take any chances." He sounded serious.

He lit one torch and used it to light the other two. Immediately the tomb swelled with orange light and the smell of burning fuel. Gathering up his bag, he started down the tunnel again.

"Oh . . . by the way. I think I've decoded the hieroglyphs on the gold scarab," he told them.

"Is that where you were during lunch today?" Kasha inquired. Her long shadow folded against the wall.

Up ahead, Elliot's hat nodded in reply. His torch left a thin, wispy trail of black smoke that swirled around Rachel's head and rested against the low ceiling where many smoke trails had already been blazed, some recently. He pointed up at them.

"That's definitely not a good sign." A few steps later he continued. "Where was I? Oh, the scarab . . . the symbols on the scarab refer to the name 'Ipiankhu.'"

"Ipiankhu," Kasha repeated softly. "Sounds like a Middle Kingdom name."

"That's what I thought, too." He glanced over his shoulder at her with a cautious smile.

"The name 'Ankhu' shows up during that time period also," Kasha added. "There are records of a vizier of that name who assisted Pharaoh. Storehouses of grain and supplies were credited to him. Would it be possible that this Ipiankhu and Ankhu are one and the same?"

"Maybe." Elliot slowed and held his torch slightly higher. "Better yet, maybe they both refer to the Egyptian name given to Joseph. As Pharaoh's right-hand man, he built warehouses to store food in anticipation of seven years of poor crops. Good thing, too.

All of Egypt, and Joseph's family as well, probably would have starved to death without his stored grain."

A final bend in the catacomb passageway revealed Rachel's 'treasure room' beyond. Lit up by the torches, its contents flashed gold and bronze.

"Goodness Agnes!" Elliot exclaimed. His satchel slid from his shoulder but he didn't seem to notice. Instead, it dragged behind him and nearly caught in his kite-string lifeline. The torchlight exposed the messy condition of the room. Artifacts were stacked one upon another, some lay strewn near a wall, others lay on the mudbrick as if dropped in a hurry.

"This . . ." Elliot's words squeezed into a hush. A sudden brightness seemed to surround them, as if someone had opened the curtains on a dark room. Silently, he motioned them into the treasure room. As they entered, their torchlight entered with them—but the orange glow remained in the catacombs.

"Torches," Kasha said quietly.

Elliot's face tensed.

"We've got company."

CHAPTER 12

"What shall we do?" Rachel's first reaction was to stuff both thumbs into her pockets so they would be safe from the approaching mummy thieves.

"First, we ditch these." Elliot collected the burning torches and snuffed them out against one wall. The room went from near daylight to almost total darkness. "This room seems to be their storeroom. I imagine they're headed here."

"Then we must leave," Kasha declared.

Elliot led them from the room and made a quick right turn.

"What are you doing!" Rachel scolded. "Isn't the entrance the other way?"

He gave her a short, blunt answer: "Uh-huh. But so are those burning torches."

They navigated the catacomb for half a minute until Elliot motioned them into a small opening in the mud-brick wall. All three squeezed, one at a time, into the narrow crevice. Elliot squeezed in last. Standing with her back to the wall, Rachel almost had to hold her

breath to avoid scraping against the opposite wall.
There was no room to turn around. Torchlight outside
the hallway flickered in and out as each torchbearer
moved from catacomb to catacomb. Then her cousin's
hushed voice echoed into the tight space.

"We've got to split up."

"What?" Rachel said in a fierce whisper. "You're the
one who said we must stick together!"

"That was before our company arrived. Now we
switch to Plan 'B.'"

"Which is?" Rachel pressed.

"I'm working on it."

A flutter of light appeared in the catacomb. It lit
Elliot's face just enough for Rachel to see behind his
gold-rimmed glasses. His gaze jumped from her eyes
to Kasha's.

"Your job," he directed both of them, "is to get back
to the entrance—any entrance—and go for help."

"Where do you think *you're* going?" challenged
Rachel.

He shrugged. "To find Plan 'B.'"

He forced his hand into his vest and withdrew a
pocket-knife. In one smooth motion, he pulled his kite-
string to one side, doubled it over and slipped the knife
blade through its loop. The string dropped limply to
the floor.

Rachel's heart jumped into her throat. Kasha, however,
helped him slip out of his shoulder bags.

"How will we find you?" Kasha asked calmly.

"Don't worry about me. I'll find my way." He fumbled
with the shoulder bag in the tight space. "Here," he

said, handing Kasha one of the two walkie-talkies. "You two hang onto this. I'll keep the other one." He gathered the extinguished torches under his arm, then adjusted his hat. The flickering torchlight grew ever closer. "See you up top." He inched his way out into the catacomb and glanced quickly in both directions. Suddenly he leaned his hatted head back into the narrow space. "Don't let Rachel eat all of the candy bars," he grinned, and was gone.

Rachel stood stone-silent. The light moved away from the hallway where they hid like sardines. Faint voices, magnified by the hollow catacomb passageways, ricocheted up through the tomb.

"What does he think he is doing!" Rachel bristled.

"Shhhhhh!" Kasha held her hand against Rachel's arm for a long minute until the torchlight melted away and the voices disappeared. Then she slung Elliot's bags over her shoulder.

"We must return to the entrance." She tugged at Rachel's kite string, then her own, to ensure they still had a way home. "Now . . . we go," she said softly.

Rachel followed her from the tight hall space into the catacomb. Several passageways led away from their hiding place. Instinctively, Kasha headed down one, but Rachel paused to pull against her twine to be sure they had chosen the correct path. They had.

It was quite dark as they wound their way along the inner tomb walls. Rachel didn't mind an occasional stumble or bumped shin in the darkness—she much preferred it to dodging the sinister torches that moved about the tunnels. Fortunately, the glowing lights that had blocked their return path to the tomb shaft had faded—for now, at least.

"How far is it . . . to the entrance, I mean?" Rachel asked.

"Fifty, possibly seventy-five meters. Not far."

Easy for Kasha to say. She had experience wandering around in tombs. Rachel, on the other hand, had no idea where they were. With each step she twisted the slack twine around her wrist so as not to trip on her lifeline. At each catacomb intersection, Kasha paused to get new bearings before moving on. Their escape was going well . . . quite well, actually. Already Rachel imagined the two of them linking up with Elliot at the bottom of the rope, climbing easily to safety, and calling in the Egyptian military—perhaps several hundred men and an attack airplane or two—to arrest the tomb robbers and return all mummy parts to their rightful owners. During her daydream, she managed to slam into Kasha's backside. Kasha had stopped abruptly in front of her.

"Sorry about that," offered Rachel. She noticed the lights in the tunnel in front of them had brightened again. "What is it? Are we there?"

"I am afraid not." Kasha motioned ahead to the unsettling glow lighting all three of their passageway choices. Rachel squinted to see that their 'bread crumb' strings led down the center corridor, right where the torchlight burned brightest.

She whispered in Rachel's ear. "Stay here."

Kasha handed Rachel the walkie-talkie and the flashlight and moved down the corridor toward the lighted tunnels. When she reached the spot where the tunnels came together, she tiptoed lightly and peeked around one wall. Several moments passed before Rachel got a signal to follow. They discovered that the tomb robbers had hung a torch in a wall bracket, marking the tunnel intersection. Further down, another torch was suspended from the wall, lighting the entire passage that would lead them up and out of the tomb.

"They are nearby," she said, motioning to the torches. "As long as these torches . . ."

A low scraping sound followed by a muffled thud rumbled from a room ahead. Kasha's eyes grew wider and darker. A short silence followed, and then was broken by voices speaking in short, sharp Arabic phrases. A bustle of activity and the noise of stone grinding against mudbrick accompanied three men out into the catacomb passage. Swiftly, Rachel bolted backwards, flattening herself into the shadow of the catacomb. Kasha pressed behind a stone pillar opposite her.

"They're coming this way!" Rachel mouthed to her companion. Kasha nodded, letting Rachel know she understood. It was too dangerous to whisper, so they spoke with hand signals.

Kasha directed Rachel toward a passageway immediately behind her. She then motioned to herself and pointed to where she would be hiding . . . somewhere down the opposite tunnel. Rachel immediately shook her head 'No!' but Kasha had already slipped away to hide. Rachel figured she should do the same, before she became mummy meat.

Unwinding her string from around her wrist as she

went, Rachel inched back in the shadows—away from the torch glow—to a nearby room. It was completely empty and looked to be a perfect place to be captured. She inched still further to a second room which appeared more promising. In the dimness she could barely make out a large stone block and a mixture of other artifacts scattered about. She quickly stepped into the room only to make two horrifying discoveries. First, she found she was sharing the room with a wooden mummy case—a sarcophagus—lying on the stone block. And, worse, she tugged at her string, only to find it snapped. Her lifeline to the entrance had vanished.

With her heart beating wildly, Rachel dived behind the block of stone, knocking over a large jar as she landed. The lid of the jar rolled a little ways away, allowing Rachel to see some cloth bundled up inside. She pulled herself to a sitting position, and cautiously removed the cloth from its container. Maybe, disguised as a linen artifact, she would escape discovery. But the cloth was too small to cover her and instead fell to one side. Then she saw what it really was . . . a robe. A long-sleeved robe of well-worn wool gathered into a heap beneath the mummy case—a fine piece of ancient clothing that just happened to match the strip of cloth she found in the 'treasure room.' And, if Elliot's facts were correct, this had to be Joseph's richly ornamented coat!

A scuffle in the catacomb quickly drew her attention. Two shadows flashed on the wall just outside the room, and two people came into view. One was a grungy man in a robe and turban. The other . . . was Elliot. His hat was missing, his glasses hanging at an angle. The robed thief had Elliot in his grasp, half-dragging, half-pushing him through the catacomb passage. The pair passed the room entrance and the noise of their struggle faded away.

Crouched in the darkness, Rachel fumbled in despair for something—anything—with which to defend herself. Several Canopic jars stood beside a low stone table. These were what Elliot had told her were used to hold the internal organs of the mummies. She wasn't about to bonk some thief over the head with a 3,000-year-old liver. She continued to search the floor behind her. At last her fingers curled around a golden cup, just right for serving up a large spot of tea. Oh, how she wished she were back at the mission house right now, listening for the teakettle's familiar whistle! She pulled the cup close, drew a slow breath, and waited—although she wasn't sure what she was waiting for. Elliot had been captured. Kasha was missing. It soon would be dark outside. And, to her knowledge, no one from the dig knew about this outbuilding or knew they were trapped in a tomb below it. All of this mystery and adventure business were one thing . . . but mummy-eating tomb robbers were something else indeed.

Five minutes passed. An occasional torch glow brightened then faded outside the room entrance, but the small nook behind the bulky sarcophagus seemed an ideal hiding spot. Rachel drew her knees to her chest and gathered the arms of the flowing robe around her to chase away the goosebumps. The chill of the mudbrick tomb was beginning to seep into her bones. And suddenly, with the ancient wool robe about her waist, she understood how Joseph must have felt when he was left in the well by his brothers to die. Being rescued—if only to be sold as a slave—might not have seemed so bad at the time. In fact, it sounded pretty good to Rachel at the moment. Things couldn't get any worse. . .

Then they did. The unearthly squeaking noise returned. Faint and muffled, it appeared to come from inside the sarcophagus just above her—and it definitely was not mice. It sounded instead like two tiny metal clips clicking against one another. She imagined the worst . . . mummy eyelids opening and closing, mummy teeth chattering, an impatient mummy drumming his fingernails on the inside of his final resting box. Tomb robbers or no tomb robbers, it was time to get out of there.

Tucking the robe sleeves into her shorts, Rachel struggled to her feet. The golden tea cup was clenched in one hand, her flashlight locked in the other. The walkie-talkie poked from her waist pack. She squirmed past the head of the sarcophagus and saw that the lid was ajar . . . ajar enough for someone to crawl into . . . or out of. Her blood ran icy as she forced herself to move the flashlight above the open mummy case. With a shaky thumb, she pressed the button. An instant beam of light poured into the wooden coffin—the *empty* wooden coffin. A loud sigh of relief escaped her lips.

"It will take more than an empty box to frighten me!" she whispered aloud to herself. Then, as if testing Rachel's resolve, a fist-sized tangle of black scurried across the floor of the sarcophagus and entered her beam of light. The squeaks that had haunted her since her first visit to the tomb now took on solid form. Two eight-legged creatures battled before her eyes. With each thrust of their stinging tails, their bodies collided, creating an oily squeaking sound that made Rachel's skin crawl.

Scorpions!

The flashlight tumbled from her shaking hand into the bottom of the hollow sarcophagus.

Arms and hands trembling, she pressed the walkie-talkie to her lips and practically screamed out a whisper.

"Elliot! Kasha! Where are you?" She released the walkie-talkie button, but no one replied.

Far beyond the mummy room entrance a dull orange glimmer appeared. From its dancing motion, Rachel knew it must be a torch. The changing light grew brighter and sharper until at last she heard footsteps moving the torchlight closer and closer. So . . . this is how it would end. She would be the lead story on the evening telly news: 'Hyena's Mound claims three young victims . . . details at ten o'clock.' Then a picture would flash up on the screen—Elliot's borrowed dig hat with two black, greasy scorpions fighting over it. The news report would be announced in Arabic, of course, so no one at the mission house, including Uncle Mason, would ever know the truth.

After a brief moment of terror she straightened her stance, adjusted her hat, and accepted her fate. First Elliot, then Kasha, now her. She could hide no longer. She had held out to the bitter end against thieves and scorpions. Now she would endure her capture with bravery and honor.

Shuffling feet drew nearer, the torchlight radiated. A long, dark shadow cast its way along the mummy room floor. Without warning, the burning torch swooped into the room followed by a dusty robe and a turban-covered head. A strong hand grasped her wrist. Rachel pinched out an uncontrolled gasp and held up a fistful of candy bars.

"Oh! Oh . . . please don't harm me! Look! I've got candy bars! You may take them . . . take them all!"

CHAPTER 13

Yanking off her turban disguise, Kasha hung her torch in a metal wall bracket and grabbed Rachel by the shoulders.

"Kasha!" Rachel nearly slumped to the ground with relief. "It's you!"

"Have you seen Elliot?" Kasha asked quickly.

Still gathering her wits, Rachel waited for her breath to return. Finally she found her voice. "I thought you were . . ."

"Elliot . . . have you seen Elliot?" she repeated.

"Yes," she managed to gasp. "He's been captured . . . or worse."

Kasha tugged her toward the sarcophagus. "When did you last see him?"

"Only a few minutes ago, out there in the cattle comb. A man dressed as you are had him clutched about the neck." As they talked, Kasha pulled the turban back on, pushing her cascades of black hair underneath it.

"Blast him!" Rachel went on. "Running off like that,

with all of those torches and such roaming up and down this blasted tomb . . . I believe he knew he would be captured, don't you?"

"Perhaps."

"What was he thinking?" snapped Rachel. Her voice betrayed her anger and worry.

"Possibly, he was thinking of us."

Kasha's answer only made her angrier with her cousin. By striking out alone, he had guaranteed extra time for her and Kasha to escape to the entrance. He also guaranteed his own capture . . . in their place.

"He hasn't slept for nearly two days, you know," Rachel informed her. "And he missed lunch . . . reading, I suppose, or doing some other foolish thing. At any rate, he must be hungry and exhausted. I'm not surprised those robbers got him. Serves him right."

"We should return to the entrance, then, and leave the tomb," Kasha concluded slowly. "Elliot must find his own way."

"What? We shall do nothing of the sort!" She turned from Kasha with a jerk. "I'm not about to leave him down here with mummies and scorpions and all that rot. And certainly not with a handful of filthy tomb robbers whose only ambition is to . . ." She noticed a thin smile hanging on Kasha's full lips.

"What on earth are you laughing at?" Rachel fumed.

"At you," she replied softly. "I do not intend to leave Elliot here. I just wanted to be certain I could count on your help."

"Then what are we waiting for?" Rachel stuffed the gold tea cup into her waist pack. She felt a surge of courage race through her body. "You may stay here and talk with these squeaky scorpions if you wish. I, however, am going to find Mr. Pea Brain."

She marched bravely from the room but had absolutely no idea which way to go. Rather than embarrass herself in this moment of boldness, she simply picked a tunnel and strode down it, full speed ahead. Kasha followed close behind. They walked thirty meters or so then came to their first catacomb intersection. A torch glowed brightly in the wall bracket where the tunnel forked. Rachel slowed her pace in hopes that Kasha might somehow direct their next step.

"I suggest we take the left passageway," Kasha offered as they proceeded past the torch.

Rachel picked up the pace again.

"My thoughts exactly," she said with confidence. A tug from behind suddenly brought her to a halt. It was Kasha, picking up the sleeve of the robe. Without a word, Kasha guided her to a spot beneath the torchlight and held the robe sleeves out to either side of Rachel's waist.

"The robe . . . it is exquisite!"

It truly was an amazing piece of clothing. Rachel hadn't bothered to examine it too closely. She had been a bit busy, what with tomb robbers searching her out for a good thumb removal as she sat spectator to the scorpion matches.

Kasha's nimble fingers ran up and down the portion of the robe dangling below Rachel's backside. As the fabric rumpled in her hands, the striking patterns of color and design moved as if alive. A row of tassels lined the robe's edges and the colorful stripes of blue and red and purple were more impressive than those on the belt Rachel had discovered earlier. In several spots along the sleeves and down its front, groups of dark, irregular spots appeared. They looked to be stains of some sort.

"This belongs to the belt you found in the treasure room?"

"I suppose it does." Rachel gently held the sleeves up from either side of her waist. "Do you really believe this could be the fancy coat of that slave boy Joseph, the one who became best buddies with some pharaoh 9 million years ago?"

Kasha's analytical eyes studied the cloth for a long moment. "Yes. By all accounts, it appears to be from the same general time period. It certainly is not a pharaoh's garment. And it appears to be sized for someone of my age, or slightly older." She smoothed the cloth. "I feel certain Elliot will have an answer for us."

"Oh, he shall have an answer . . . he *always* has an answer!" Rachel took several steps away from the wall torch into a safer area of catacomb shadows. "And speaking of Mr. Answer, what shall we do . . . when we find Elliot, I mean?"

"We must occupy the attention of the robbers long enough to free him." Kasha answered as if she had already planned the entire escape. She looked steadily into Rachel's eyes. "Do you recall telling me I should be a sister of Elliot?"

"Yes, quite. And I do apologize . . . I wouldn't wish that horrible fate on anyone."

"In order to free Elliot, you and I must now become sisters."

"I've never had a sister. I'm not certain I'd know just what to do with one. What exactly do sisters do to one another?"

"Often they argue." Kasha offered her a knowing smile. "But they also help one another. And that is how we shall free your cousin."

She proceeded to create a story—a drama of sorts—that would busy the tomb robbers while Elliot escaped. Rachel made a few adjustments to the short plot to increase her stage time. She also had to learn a couple of Arabic phrases, just in case trouble arose.

Rachel took a deep breath at the thought of what lay before them—finding Elliot, fooling the thieves with their play, and escaping to the entrance unharmed.

"Kasha," Rachel said slowly, "you know what else sisters do? They share." With that, Rachel took her candy bars out of her waist pack and handed one to Kasha. As she unwrapped one for herself, she smiled and held it up. "Here's to the rescue."

"Yes, cheers," Kasha said, smiling back. "Thank you for sharing, Rachel."

Energized by the chocolate, they followed the catacomb mazes in search of Elliot. After exploring two dead-end tunnels, they came upon a long corridor. It almost looked familiar to Rachel.

"Do you know where we are?" Kasha asked.

"Not exactly. But we've been here before, haven't we?"

Kasha waved her robed arm toward one end of the passageway. A thin shaft of light shone down on the mudbrick floor ahead. A cracked obelisk cast its shadow in their direction.

"The entrance lies there, just twenty meters beyond."

Suddenly something else caught Rachel's eye. There, in the tomb dust, lay Elliot's walkie-talkie. She bent to grab it.

"Wait! Do not touch it," Kasha advised. She approached it carefully. "I believe Elliot may have left it here as a clue . . ." She knelt and searched the dusty floor. The walkie-talkie was switched off. It lay on its back with its short antenna pointing toward a partially hidden opening in the catacomb wall. "Mmmm . . . how clever."

'Clever' was one of many words people always used to describe Elliot and his activities. Rachel was nearly sick to death of hearing it along with his name. But she had to ask anyway.

"What is it?" Then she noticed a thin line in the dust that led to the opening. The end of the line became an obvious arrow.

"They have taken him here." Kasha picked up the walkie-talkie, tightened her turban, and stepped up to enter the hidden corridor. Glancing back over her shoulder, she made a suggestion. "It is best that we look like tomb robbers. You also should wear a robe, but not the one you found. It is too precious."

Rachel untucked the robe from her waist and slipped the garment in the canvas bag of Elliot's that she was still carrying, exchanging it for another dusty garment that Kasha held out to her. She salvaged what remained of her kite-string and used it to cinch the robe at her waist. The robe was a bit long and scratchy, but it was much better than looking like a British tourist lost in a hidden tomb hideout.

"There," Kasha said, half smiling. "Now we really look like sisters."

She followed Kasha through the opening, which narrowed slightly before widening again. It wasn't long until Rachel heard the low echo of voices ahead. The warm glow of torchlight spilling from a room ahead lit the path before them. Gradually Kasha slowed to a stop. They had reached a wide opening that served as an opening to a slightly sunken cavern-like room.

The room was larger than most they had encountered. A domed ceiling rose nearly three meters above the mudbrick floor. Several small cubby-hole rooms connected to it and in the one farthest from them sat a bound and gagged Elliot, his sandy hair mussed to one side. Three tomb robbers stood in the room's center speaking what Rachel now knew to be Arabic.

"So . . . what are they saying?" she quizzed Kasha.

The Egyptian girl listened a moment.

"They have friends arriving soon," she whispered. "They intend to move more artifacts in tonight, when the Austrians turn off the generator lights at Tell ed-Daba." She listened a moment longer and a look of distress crossed her bronzed face. "We need to distract them so that we may free Elliot."

"A distraction? You need a distraction? Well, distraction is my specialty. I practice on Elliot all the time."

She sized up the thieves before them. "They look relatively harmless . . ."

"Look again." Kasha pointed out a long knife sheathed in the belt of one robber. Another drew a short blade which he proceeded to use on his teeth like a toothpick. Rachel felt her shoulders shrink at the sound of cold steel scraping against grimy teeth. He sounded like a walkie-talkie with a button problem.

"That's it!" Rachel gasped softly, grabbing Kasha's arm. "The walkie-talkies . . . we can distract them with the walkie-talkies!"

"What do you mean?"

"It's quite simple, actually. I've fooled Mother this way a number of times . . . not that it takes much to fool someone like Mother, who only pays attention to herself . . ." Rachel reached into her robe, peeled open her waist pack, and turned on her walkie-talkie. She motioned for Kasha to do the same with Elliot's unit. After a quick search of the area leading into the domed room, she selected the perfect spot, down a far corridor. "Can you sneak down that tunnel and hide a walkie-talkie behind the pile of artifacts in that cattle comb? I have a marvelous idea."

Cautiously Kasha made her way down the corridor to the artifact pile, maneuvering behind large rocks, cracked obelisks and stone walls spattered with hieroglyphs. Rachel watched from her hiding spot near the large room's entrance.

"This one's for you, Mother," Rachel announced under her breath.

Kasha placed the walkie-talkie amid a stack of clay

pots and assorted ancient weapons hidden deep in the corridor. Several tense minutes passed as she made her way back to their hiding spot overlooking the open room.

"Now," Rachel told her, "you talk into here, and they will hear you over there." She pointed to the other walkie-talkie. Kasha smiled.

"This must be why Elliot says you are an expert snoop," Kasha complimented her.

"He told you that, did he?" Rachel felt a tiny bubble of anger rise in her chest. Elliot was right, of course. But he should have told her face-to-face instead of blabbing it to Kasha. Come to think of it, he *had* told her she was a snoop. "Well . . . this 'snoop' is about to save his dirt-digger skin."

Kasha lifted the second walkie-talkie from Rachel's hand. "Are you certain you are ready?"

Rachel nodded but couldn't speak. Her mouth had gone completely dry. Looking into the domed room, she tried to remember exactly what Kasha had taught her to say, and whispered it to herself under her breath.

The three tomb robbers were now scattered about the room, two sitting on one side and the third leaning against the tomb's mudbrick wall opposite them. Elliot's feet poked from his small cubbyhole just beyond the third robber. If all went according to plan, the hidden walkie-talkie would lure the robbers away from their post . . . leaving Rachel a short time to dash in and free Elliot. If, however, the thieves proved smarter than they looked, the original rescue would be set in motion. Rachel would surprise the three with her presence, then Kasha would distract them while Elliot was set free. Timing and acting were important. If anything went wrong, they would all be captured. The tomb's hidden treasures would be lost forever, as would the three of them.

Kasha bobbed her turban-tied head as if to signal their last chance at escape. Her finger squeezed the walkie-talkie button and she pressed it close to her lips.

"Duktoor! 'Ayza duktoor!"

Doctor! I want a doctor! It was one of several phrases Kasha had taught her moments earlier. That should do the trick—hearing some poor Egyptian girl hollering for help ought to make anyone scramble . . . even tomb robbers. And that it did.

The two thieves opposite Elliot jumped immediately. One pulled a long knife from his waist belt and fell in behind the second robber. Both swarmed up the low incline into the corridor, led by Kasha's voice toward the walkie-talkie hidden in the tunnel. Kasha clicked the button off.

"So far, so good," she whispered to Rachel.

Unfortunately, the third robber who was guarding Elliot had no intention of leaving his spot. He stood motionless, leaning against the wall only meters away from his prisoner. Thirty seconds passed and still he held his post. Rachel realized that only one option remained.

"Two down, one to go," she murmured. "The others will return any moment when they discover that their injured Egyptian girl is really a walkie-talkie. We've got to do something." Kasha's tense expression told Rachel she was right.

She tested the makeshift twine belt around her waist, making sure it would hold the oversized robe closed so she wouldn't trip. Kasha helped adjust Rachel's robe and whispered into her ear:

"Remember . . . you are the actress. This is the stage. They must believe you are my ill sister."

With one final, deep breath Rachel stepped from her shoes, held up the robe so she wouldn't trip, and stumbled, headlong and barefoot, into the center of the tomb room.

CHAPTER 14

"*Ha moot! Ha moot, ha moot!*" she cried, over and over again. This was one of several handy little phrases she had learned from Kasha . . . it meant 'I feel like I'm about to die.' As she wailed she spun in a tight circle that moved her ever closer to Elliot's cubbyhole jail.

The startled thief stood at attention. Clearly, he did not expect a crazed girl to spin her way into the tomb. He seemed surprised and genuinely puzzled as to what to do. Rachel seized her advantage and played it to the fullest, mingling short hoots and screeches with her limited Arabic vocabulary. The shocked face of the tomb robber simply fueled her theatrical fire.

"*Ana ta'baana,*" she sighed, rolling her eyes. A practiced stagger led her directly into the thief's torchlight. "*Ana ta'baana,*" she repeated, Arabic for 'I'm tired.' *This has got to work!* she thought.

With one final jerk she dropped limply to the mud-brick floor. Her head flopped backwards, flinging part of her hair across her face. She came to rest less than a meter from Elliot's feet. As her eyelids fluttered in one last dramatic convulsion, she managed a wink in his direction. Even with a strip of cloth tied across his mouth, Elliot's stunned look of disbelief was unmistakable. Then she forced one last breath:

"Anna banana . . . who ate my banana?" It wasn't exactly Arabic, but it would do.

Now it was Kasha's turn. Rachel heard her footstep patting across the hard floor toward her. The lone robber who had stood up upon Rachel's entrance, now approached Kasha. Through the corner of her eye, Rachel saw Kasha holding him captive with her charm, beauty, and heart-felt concern for her 'sister's' health.

"My poor sister!" she sobbed in Arabic. She launched into the long, sad story of how her sister came to be so ill, how the family had no money, how she soon would die without medical treatment . . . even recounting the horrible tale of her sister's fall into this awful tomb in the first place. All of this was in Arabic, of course, so Rachel didn't understand a single word. But she had helped write the story so she knew the basic plot. She also knew the ending—if this little masquerade didn't work, she, Kasha, and Elliot would become permanent fixtures in this stale tomb.

While Kasha distracted the thief, Rachel inched slowly across the floor toward Elliot. Although his feet were free, his hands were tied behind his back. The cloth gag across his face looked extremely uncomfortable. As she reached him he rolled to one side, pulled his tied hands under his legs and over his shoes, bringing them to the front of his body, and clambered to his feet. Rachel tore wildly at the rope binding his hands but it wouldn't loosen.

"Mmphf!" Elliot motioned to the cloth gag.

"We haven't time for that!" she hissed. "Come on!"

She pulled him from the cubbyhole and both ran toward a corridor leading away from the open room. She glanced over her shoulder just in time to see Kasha pretend to faint as they made their escape. It was quite a good faint, actually. The tomb robber watched her topple to the floor. But the sound of their escaping footsteps drew his attention too soon and he cried out at them, waving his fists.

"Now we've done it!" Rachel groaned.

"Mmphf! Mmphf!"

Rachel held a finger in Elliot's face. "Not a word. Just follow me as quickly as you can."

She slipped between a pair of crumbling obelisks and into the nearest catacomb, then sped toward the shaft of light waiting at its end. Elliot lumbered behind, working at freeing his tied hands. "That won't do, you know! You've got to move faster than that!" she warned over her shoulder.

Finally she reached the narrowed opening where they had found Elliot's walkie-talkie. But when she turned to pull Elliot through and into the entrance passageway, he wasn't there.

"Blast you, Elliot Conner!" she yelled into the echoing catacomb. "I've risked both thumbs rescuing you from these mummy cattle combs! I shan't do it again, do you hear me? Do you?"

Frantic footsteps pounded in the distant passageway. Rachel quickly pressed her back against the wall in a useless attempt to hide. Her chest heaved with each gasp for breath. How foolish of her to call out in this hollow tomb! She had given herself away.

The outline of a body running toward her with a bag slung around its neck and a lantern swinging from both hands appeared. Instinctively, she grabbed for the flashlight in her waist pack but her hand only found candy bar wrappers. So she waited, motionless. The person drew closer, the footsteps louder. Then, in the bouncing lantern light, she recognized the form as Elliot's. When he reached her, he practically threw the lantern at her feet. He then swooped to his knees and, with hands still tied together, he turned the wick handle and smothered the lantern's flame.

"Mmphf!"

Rachel pulled the satchel from his neck and yanked at the cloth gag still strapped about his mouth. It loosened just enough to drop to his neck. He was panting hard, pulling for air, as if his next words would be the most important Rachel might ever hear. With one deep breath he gazed up at her through the smudges on his glasses and spoke.

"Anna Banana?"

"It worked, didn't it? You're free, aren't you?" She glared at him. "I believe I liked you the way you were before . . . with a cloth stuffed around your mouth."

He drew a second breath. "Where's Kasha?"

"I thought you had gone to rescue her!"

Elliot stared at the mudbrick floor for several long moments.

"I've got to go find her." He struggled to his feet and

clutched at his head to adjust his dirt-digger hat—which wasn't there. "Goodness Agnes! They've still got my hat!"

"We shall leave this rot here and grab it on our way out of this place," Rachel said hurriedly. "Come on, then. Kasha may need our help."

"Wait! My hands." Elliot held out his hands, still tied together at the wrists. "There's a pocketknife in my vest." Once she retrieved the knife, it took Rachel several tries to find a cutting blade. In the process she discovered a corkscrew, a compass, and complete set of silverware. Finally the knife blade unfolded and, after a few slices with the sharp blade, Elliot was free.

"We must be close to our tomb entrance," he observed. "I think this is where the tomb robbers brought me in."

"Right. We go through this narrow opening, make a left . . . or is it a right . . . it doesn't matter! We can see the light from the entrance once we climb through."

"Kasha must still be back in the cavern. We might be able to . . ." He stopped to listen.

More frantic footsteps pounded in the distant passageway. But these were not the footsteps of a lively Egyptian girl. They were the stampede of tomb robber feet heading toward them from the cavern room.

"Looks as though we'll have to find another way." Rachel tossed the shoulder bag through the narrow opening then followed it through. Reluctantly, Elliot did the same.

"I've got a pretty good map in my head of this tomb maze," he thought aloud. "There are at least two other ways to circle back to the cavern. One has wall torches and one is dark. The dark route is longer but safer."

The sound of clomping footsteps nearly drowned him out. Rachel knew it was reckless to go deeper into the tomb when they were so close to their escape entrance. From this spot, they could both climb the rope and be gone in only a few minutes—and leave Kasha behind. Suddenly she realized she would rather be captured than leave her friend. Together they turned toward the catacombs leading back through the ancient city of the dead. But a voice pulled them back.

"Where are you going?"

A tall silhouette with cascades of black hair called out to them from the shafted tomb entrance at the tunnel's end.

"This way!" Kasha's welcome voice echoed again down the catacomb.

Rachel spun around and bolted toward the cascading hair but Elliot dropped to one knee.

"Wait!" he cried.

"Wait?" Rachel went numb. "Perhaps you haven't been alive the past few minutes, but there are thumb-eating mummy crunchers dashing down that passage-way just waiting to get their hands on the likes of you! Kasha's here, I'm here. Tell *them* to wait if you wish. We're climbing out of here! Now!"

"Give me a hand!" Elliot had both hands wrapped around the lantern.

"What on earth are you doing!"

"Buying time! Hurry!"

Rachel whisked back to his side. Kasha followed her,

the bag and its precious contents still hanging from her shoulder.

"Look back into the opening we climbed through . . . can you see them—all of them?" he pressed her.

"Yes, yes! The three of them! They're coming! Do something!"

Elliot unscrewed the base of the metal kerosene lantern. With several quick swings he spattered the smelly fuel along the floor, down the passageway, around and up both sides of the narrow opening. Pulling Rachel's tomb-robber robe to one side, he thrust his hand into her waist pack and flipped out a small foil packet of matches. The thieves pounded closer, their footsteps booming in time to the heart-beats in Rachel's chest. Elliot reached to strike a match on the mudbrick wall . . . then froze. His gaze fell upon the cloth sleeve dangling from Kasha's bag.

"What are you waiting for!" Rachel screeched.

He adjusted his glasses with his free hand, looking at her with astonishment. Suddenly his ungagged jaw dropped open. The lantern fell. He clamped his hands onto her arms.

"The| . . . the robe. Joseph's robe! It's . . . it's . . ."

"I believe the word you're looking for is 'exquisite.'" Rachel remarked. He nodded, speechless. "Don't ask me how I knew that. I'm a mind reader. And at this moment, I'm seeing a complete blank in that shriveled brain of yours. We haven't time for archeological twit-ter over this old coat! Get on with it!"

Elliot dragged the match down the wall with one long stroke. It sparked to life. Carefully, he flicked it into the narrow opening. Instantly, the entire space before them exploded with an enormous *Whoosh!* of fire. A sharp blast of heated air jumped across Rachel's face as the flames climbed their way around the entire opening, sealing the tomb robbers on the other side of the wall of fire.

"That should hold them for a while! Let's go!" Elliot yelled.

They turned away from the flaming opening toward Kasha, who had raced ahead of them toward the entrance. Just as they reached her, the three tomb robbers encountered the fire. Their angry shouts bounced through the passageway.

"Quickly!" said Kasha. The three of them rushed on toward the dim shaft of rectangular light bathing the tomb floor just below the entrance where Rachel had fallen only hours earlier. Elliot, as always, was one step ahead. He called out instructions as they neared the shaft.

"It'll take the robbers a couple of minutes to circle back through the cavern. As soon as we climb out, we've got to reseal this entrance. Rachel, you can help Kasha tie the rope around the big stone slab. I'll loop the rope over the ceiling hook to make a pulley, just like we did earlier. We'll slide it back into place then go for help."

Rachel spit into her palms, preparing for the climb that would lead her to safety. Knowing that the thieves would be there soon gave her the extra energy she needed to make the climb. As she reached out to grasp the rope, her hands found nothing but stale tomb air.

One quick look at her feet sent a merciless chill up her spine. There, on the mudbrick floor, lay the rope—their only means of escape—in a tattered, scratchy heap.

CHAPTER 15

"Goodness Agnes!"

Elliot's put his hand to his head, squinting as he thought of their predicament.

"This does not look good," Kasha said in her calm, steady way. She stood looking up the shaft with the rope puddled at her feet. Her face took on the same expression Elliot's did when faced with a mental challenge. Even her cat-eye squint resembled his own. "I believe it can be climbed."

Immediately Elliot joined her in the rope puddle and looked toward the opening above.

"I think you're right. One of us wall-steps up and ties off the rope. Then the other two climb to safety."

Rachel couldn't believe her ears.

"*I* think you are both absolutely insane! What would one climb on? Mummy dust? There is nothing to hold!" Rachel felt herself fully qualified to attack their idea, having climbed her share of trees back in England, usually when Mother was searching for her.

"You climb like this." Elliot pushed one hand against

the tomb wall and lifted his leg to illustrate his point. "The pressure from your hands and feet against the walls holds you in place. As you shift the pressure, you force your body higher."

"I think not."

"It's sort of like climbing the center of a jungle gym," Elliot explained. "I've climbed shafts like this one before."

"When?" she challenged.

"In the basement at school, rescuing bird eggs from a nest in the furnace shaft. I got sent to the principal's office for doing it, but it worked. Now . . . I can lift you . . ."

"*You?*" Rachel gasped in disbelief. "You, Elliot Conner, Mr. Perfect, did something you weren't supposed to do? And got caught? Oh, how absolutely splendid! I wish I could have been there to see that wire-rimmed face of yours! I must meet this teacher, you know. I've got a few things to tell . . ."

He covered her mouth with an urgent hand.

"If we're not out of here in . . ." He checked his fancy watch. ". . . in five minutes, it won't matter. None of us will ever see another teacher." Elliot helped Rachel out of her robe and stuck it in his bag, freeing her arms and legs so she could move easily.

"When you reach the top, I'll toss you what's left of the rope. Tie one end around the edge of the stone slab and drop the other end down to us."

"I've got a better idea, Mr. Bird Nest!" she snapped back. "*You* inch your way up this thing and we shall throw the rope to you!"

Elliot eyed the shaft.

"Look . . . the only way to get someone up into this shaft is to lift him." One quick look told Rachel he was right. And she knew she wouldn't be lifting Elliot up above her shoulders. Neither would Kasha. "That's why you have to go first," he finished. "Now, climb up, would you?" He made his hands into a stirrup for Rachel to climb on.

"Oh, why must I always be first!" Rachel muttered. She put one hand on his shoulder and put her foot in Elliot's locked hands. She reached her arms up against the inside of the shaft for balance while he tried to hold her steady below.

"Okay!" he grunted. "I'm going to lift. And when I do, you've got to push your hands and feet against the inner walls of the shaft. Ready?"

Rachel scanned Kasha's face. Kasha gave her a confident nod then reached out to help steady her.

"I'm ready," Rachel said quietly. Moments later her head rose into the shaft. She pressed both hands flat to the walls. Next she swung her free foot sideways until it came into contact with the shaft.

"Here goes!" Elliot heaved a final time, giving her a split second to pop her foot free from his hand-hold and slam it against the wall of the inner shaft. Suddenly she found herself suspended in mid-air, two meters from the floor—in nearly the same spot she fell from earlier. Her hands and feet stuck to the walls as if plastered there with gigantic wads of gum. There was just enough room to keep her knees and elbows bent slightly for support.

"Are you steady?" Elliot's voice came from somewhere below. She couldn't look down for fear of losing her footing. She could only look straight ahead at the mudbrick wall.

"I believe so."

"Now . . . inch your way up the shaft. Shift your weight from one side to the other, always pressing up. Like a four-legged spider. Can you do that?"

The tense ring to his voice told her they were losing precious time. Elliot and Kasha still had to climb out, and the tomb robbers were no longer yelling at the narrow opening. They had begun their trek through the cavern room. Time was precious indeed.

"I hate spiders!" she called down to him.

"Then pretend there's a giant one chasing you, and hurry up!"

Kasha's voice chimed in behind his. "You can do it, Rachel."

After drawing a deep breath, she made her first move. She strained with her left leg and slowly slid her left hand up the wall several inches. So far, so good. But she knew the pressing and sliding motions had to come naturally, without thinking. Almost like a game. Otherwise, she would freeze up or, worse yet, slip to the floor below. Then a nasty thought struck her. She stopped her climb and called down.

"What if the rope won't reach? What if it is too short?"

"Then I'll lift Kasha up to help you," Elliot's voice rang around her. His answer still didn't explain how he would escape. "You've got to have faith, Rachel—just like Joseph. He never gave up on himself, his family, or his God. We'll all make it out of here!"

"Oh really?" She pushed hard against the shaft walls with her flattened hands. "The only part of Joseph that left Egypt was his bones!"

"But he ruled here for years and saved thousands of people from starvation! That's what counts!"

He did have a point.

Rachel certainly hoped they would escape, although she didn't have Elliot's unshakeable confidence. Nor his faith. Somehow, just knowing *he* had both gave her the extra strength to go on. She resumed her climb. Now she needed something to take her mind off their dismal situation. It would be dark by now, or nearly so. The bright stars above Egypt would be appearing in the wide, open sky. Perhaps Uncle Mason had sent out a search party . . .

Before she knew it, Rachel had found a climbing rhythm, shifting her weight, pushing off, shifting again. All went quite smoothly until she felt her hand slip. She held her breath and pushed out at the walls with both arms and legs. Her knees locked into place. She strained to keep the muscles in her legs from shaking, as beads of sweat formed on her upper lip and forehead.

"You owe me one, Elliot Conner!" she called to the wall in front of her, not daring to look down. "I wouldn't do this just for you, you know. If not for Kasha, you would be out hiring a monkey to complete this climb!"

She couldn't see him, but she imagined Elliot to adjust his glasses while casting a glance of confusion toward Kasha. Kasha, however, answered as though she understood Rachel's words.

"I will see that he treats us all to ice cream once we have reached home." Her answer was all Rachel needed—a reassuring voice. It floated up the shaft, filling her with hope.

"Fine!" Rachel inched another step. "But I would much prefer a good chocolate bar!" What she said didn't matter. What really mattered was that someone besides herself—Kasha and Elliot to be exact—cared if she made it. It gave her the energy to go on. More importantly, she was concerned about them.

Only a few weight-shifts later, Rachel had nearly reached the top.

"If I can just . . . reach . . . the top . . . edge . . ." With each word, she grunted out the few final finger-lengths that led her to the opening in the floor of the mudbrick building. At last she felt her fingers curl around the lip of the entrance. One hard shove with her arms brought her legs up from beneath her and onto the floor of the old building. She was free. Hurriedly, she spun around and peered down the shaft.

"Kasha! You're next! Come on!"

A moment later the bundle of rope flew up the shaft and landed with a *clomp* beside her. Elliot's flashlight followed.

"Tie it off!" Elliot's voice rang in her ears. "Hurry!"

The darkness of the mudbrick building made Rachel's task much more difficult. She fumbled with the flashlight, propped it opposite the stone slab for light, and swiftly looped the rope around the slab, securing it with a tight knot. A quick shove with her foot sent the rope's other end falling freely down the shaft. Then she shone the flashlight into the tomb, where the rope's end dangled less than one meter above Elliot's head.

Kasha came first, the bag hanging around her neck. She used Elliot's hand as a springboard to reach the rope, climbed a short distance hand-over-hand, then swung back and forth until her feet bounced against the shaft wall. With every bounce, she shimmied farther up the rope, drawing closer to Rachel each second. Her hands grasped the edge of the opening just as the voice of one of the tomb robbers echoed through the catacombs. One hard, final pull propelled her out of the tomb and into Rachel's company.

All of their remaining equipment—stuffed into Elliot's satchel—followed on Kasha's heels. The satchel flew up the shaft into Kasha's waiting arms. The only thing left behind was Elliot. After three strong jumps, he managed to snag the swinging rope and begin his climb. He curled his feet around the scratchy cord and yanked with both hands, propelling himself upward like a sandy-haired inchworm. Rachel watched his progress from above with the flashlight trained on his every move.

Suddenly a brief commotion erupted somewhere beneath him. Another tomb robber's voice became clear. Then the third. The faint glimmer of torchlight appeared in the catacomb, throwing Elliot's inchworm shadow along the upper shaft wall. The torchlight loomed brighter with his every wiggle.

"Hurry, Elliot!" Kasha wrapped her hands around the rope to steady it and winced with pain as its scratchy twine twisted in her palms. The higher Elliot climbed, the brighter the torchlight grew. Rachel seized the rope, too; her hands clutched next to Kasha's. Together they watched Elliot fight against gravity. With no sleep and no food, Rachel feared he might not make it.

Three dark faces appeared at the shaft's bottom, accompanied by loud and angry shouts. One of the thieves jumped, snatched the loose end of the rope, and jerked it wildly side to side. Elliot held tightly. Only a few feet remained between him and Kasha's outstretched hand.

"Hold on!" Rachel shouted, releasing her grip on the rope. She reached for the flashlight and heaved the thing straight down at the hollering group below. It zipped past Elliot's scalp, missing him by a hair. A howl rang out as the flashlight bounced off the top of one thief's turban.

"Put *that* on your mummy menu!" Rachel cried out.

For a long moment all fell silent. Then a faint crackling sound drifted up the shaft. The glow of the torches took on a sharp edge, sparks scattering like a kindled fire. Curls of smoke rose from the opening. They had set the rope aflame!

Swiftly Elliot pulled himself the last meter. With Kasha's help, he crawled from the shaft just as a tongue of yellow flame completely engulfed the rope.

"Run! Now!" he yelled. He grabbed Rachel and pulled her toward the outbuilding door. She wrestled herself away long enough to call down the shaft one final time.

"So sorry! I nearly forgot your dessert!" She thrust her crumpled candy bar wrappers down the hole, then scrambled through the doorway.

Once outside the mudbrick hut, Elliot's tired legs collapsed under him.

"I will go on," Kasha panted. "You must stay with Elliot. Stay together. Hike to the dig site as quickly as you can." With the bag over one shoulder and Elliot's satchel over the other, she ran ahead into the dusk, toward the lights burning at the excavation site.

"You heard her, then. Come on," Rachel ordered him. "I won't have you stopping to search out old pots or something, do you understand?"

He wrapped one arm around her waist for support. They followed a curving path leading back to the dig and mission buildings, walking as briskly as possible. Near the dig's edge, Elliot slowed his pace. He lowered himself on a mound to wait for the small swarm of people headed their way. Half a dozen Austrian archeologists, Uncle Mason, Dr. Ahmed, and a handful of local workers met them at the edge of the site, racing past them toward the mudbrick outbuilding in search of the tomb robbers. Kasha followed behind them. When she reached the mound she dropped on her knees next to Elliot.

"They know what has happened. They are on their way to capture the thieves and save the artifacts."

Elliot, panting and exhausted, gave Kasha a gratetul nod.

"Oh, I found these in the tomb," Kasha went on as

she held up two hats. "I believe they are yours." Her soft eyes lit up the darkness as she handed Elliot his perfectly ugly dig hat. Rachel took the other one.

"My hat!" Elliot cried. He took it from Kasha's delicate hand and tugged it tight to his head. He gazed deeply into her shining eyes. "Thanks," he said hoarsely. Then he stood up, adjusted his hat and glasses, and gave Rachel a curious stare.

"By the way, nice robe."

"What? This old thing?" Rachel snorted. She took the bag from Kasha's shoulder and offered Elliot a smile. "You should see me in *this*," she said, opening the bag to reveal Joseph's robe. "I look exquisite!"

CHAPTER 16

EPILOGUE

"I've been thinking . . ."

Elliot stopped Rachel before she could continue.

"We're all in trouble now," he joked.

She cleared her throat loudly.

"Ahem! As I was saying before that rude interruption, I've got an idea or two for that Joseph's coat display we'll be setting up here at the SIMA museum."

"Oh, really?" As usual, Arlene, Uncle Mason's secretary at the museum, expressed a great deal of interest in Rachel's ideas. The gray-haired woman ran the museum when Uncle Mason was out on a dig and, when necessary, reminded him of that fact. Now that they were back from Egypt, Arlene busied herself with what she did best . . . keeping Uncle Mason organized. Her steel-gray eyes peeked over a pair of reading glasses, her gaze giving Rachel her complete approval. "I'd like to hear those ideas," she said, as she handed Uncle Mason a short stack of telephone messages.

"Thanks, Arlene," answered Rachel. She ignored everyone else and concentrated on Arlene's slightly wrinkled face.

"We should cut a piece of scratchy rope," Rachel began, "a few feet long, and curl it up like a snake in one of the larger display cases. Next to it we put the gold tea cup I found, a photo of me at the dig, and an account of how I was nearly killed discovering Joseph's bathrobe. The story would go something like this."

She handed Arlene a sheet of paper, with Rachel's handwriting on it, which the secretary began to read aloud.

"'Golden tea artifact and robe of Joseph, foreign ruler in Egypt. Discovered by Dr. Rachel Ashton, collector and celebrity, who risked life and thumb in the dangerous cattle combs beneath the dreadful 'Mound of the Hyena' in Egypt's Delta region. Dr. Ashton received the coveted Tomb-Seeker Award for placing herself in the jaws of death to preserve this bit of the past for our future.'"

"Tomb-Seeker Award?" repeated Uncle Mason. "Never heard of that one."

"Well, if there isn't one, there should be. And I shall be the first to receive it." Rachel rounded out her idea. "If there is room in the glass box, I suppose we could actually display the robe as well. And we shall need several stuffed scorpions, as well."

"Ah, that would be a nice touch, dearie," Arlene encouraged.

"I've also thought about a cardboard cutout," she went on. "We could have a life-sized photo of me mounted on cardboard, the type you see in movie theaters and so forth, and the robe would be displayed as if I were wearing it. Perhaps a nice string of pearls and a pair of gold slippers . . ."

Uncle Mason interrupted her brainstorming with a hearty chuckle.

"Let's wait and see what the Egyptian Museum curators in Cairo recommend. They may have some helpful ideas. I'm just pleased they'll allow us to display the robe for a time."

"They should be thankful we found all of those artifacts for them," Rachel countered. "And captured those three bungling tomb robbers."

Elliot remained curiously quiet through all of this discussion, his head buried in a two-page air mail letter bearing a Cairo postmark.

"So . . . what do you think, Pyramid Prince?" Rachel taunted him. No response. She turned to Arlene. "I imagine Elliot favors something stuffy and boring—a bit less creative—like placing the robe on a coat hanger inside a bare glass box and calling it 'Egypt's Closet.'"

Finally Elliot looked up from his letter and adjusted his precious hat.

"Actually, I thought we might use the back part of Room 3 to re-create the tomb, and fill up the space with real artifacts. No cardboard."

"Mmmm . . . Room 3," Rachel placed her finger under her chin in deep thought. "That would be the 'Rachel Ashton Display Room,' would it not?"

Elliot frowned.

"Dad's right—let's see what the experts say."

"Experts? Oh yes, yes . . . of course. You mean Kasha." She said Kasha's name slowly while giving Elliot a teasing grin. "What does she say in that letter, by the way? Or is it too personal?" Rachel caught a wink from Arlene.

"Nothing much." He glanced through the text of the letter then spoke again. "I take that back. There are a couple of things in here . . . " His eyes skimmed down the first page. Rachel was certain he would leave out the best parts. No matter—she would snoop later.

"Kasha researched the hidden tomb where we found the artifacts. It is believed to be a family tomb of some kind, maybe several families. More than likely they were families who worked for the vizier. For Joseph, that is."

"They must have been large families," Rachel observed. "Otherwise, why would they need so many rooms?"

"Apparently the underground maze was used for grain storage at one time, before being converted to a tomb. Some archeologists believe Joseph had three or four storage areas spread throughout Lower Egypt to supply the people with food during the famines. That hidden tomb may have been one of them."

"I still can't believe we found a mummy's thumb." Rachel said, her face screwed into a grimace as she thought about it.

"Oh, yeah . . . Kasha says all of the artifacts were returned to the Egyptian Museum. The golden scarab. Even the thumb. They put it back with it's rightful mummy owner."

"I can't tell Mother about the thumb, you know. She would simply croak." An interesting thought quickly crossed her mind. "Then again, maybe I *should* tell her . . ."

Arlene broke in on her not-so-ladylike thought.

"That reminds me, dearie. She called yesterday."

"Mother? What did she say? Is she coming for me?"

"Well, not exactly. She said she had an important appointment and that a man who works for her, an Owen, I believe, would pick you up tomorrow. She said you would understand."

"Oh, I understand *all* too well," Rachel huffed.

Quickly Arlene jumped in.

"But I told her we would arrange to get you back to Kentucky on the weekend. It's only a few hours' drive, and Dr. Conner always has a great deal of museum work to be done after these trips of yours. You'll be needing Rachel's help this week, won't you?" She looked at Uncle Mason.

"Absolutely!" he boomed. "Someone's got to set up the Joseph display, right?"

"Well then, that takes care of that," Rachel decided. "Thanks again, Arlene."

The spry secretary's eyes lit up the silver reading glasses above her smile.

Elliot flipped his letter from Kasha to page two.

"Dr. Ahmed sent the robe off to a colleague. They did some lab tests on those dark stains on the robe. Guess what they turned out to be?"

"Something that crawled off of your hat, perhaps?" Rachel couldn't pass up the opportunity to take a swipe at her cousin.

"I'm guessing it's blood," said Uncle Mason as he flipped through his messages.

"Right. Goat blood, to be exact. No big surprise, of course. Joseph's brothers dipped his coat in goat blood to fool his father into thinking he was dead, remember?"

Rachel jumped in.

"That is ridiculous! How could they know it is goat blood and not people blood? That coat is thousands of years old and besides . . . blood is blood—isn't it?"

Elliot smiled.

"Not exactly. Each drop they found had a tiny little patch of hair growing on its chin. And all the drops had tails and made this little *blaahhh*-ing sound."

He quickly threw his arms up to protect himself against Rachel's move to bean him with the gold tea cup. "I'm kidding!" he called out in defense. "Just take my word for it. There really is a difference!"

"What else is in that letter?" pressed Rachel.

"That's about it," he avoided. "Except for this." He held out a fragile yellow flower, dried in the Egyptian sun, and pressed flat for mailing in the air mail envelope.

"How lovely!"

"It's for me," Elliot said with a mischievous smile. "Oh, and Rachel—Kasha says to tell you hello. She says to check your e-mail. There may be a message."

"Well, that's jolly good of her, isn't it?" Rachel said, pleased.

"You can use the computer in my office, dearie," Arlene said.

As she stood to leave the room, Rachel cautioned everyone: "Now, I want no plans made on my bathrobe display until I return. I shall be back in a jiffy." She slipped into Arlene's office and closed the door. While she waited for the computer to bring up her e-mail, she pulled the last of her Egyptian candy bars from her pocket and unwrapped it. A minute later, a short note appeared on the computer screen. It had been sent while she, Elliot, and Uncle Mason were still on the airplane bound for home.

Dear Rachel,
I imagine you are low on candy bars by now. I will send more to you soon. Although I enjoy my summer job here at the Egyptian Museum, it seems less exciting now that I have experienced the true adventure of preserving the past for our future.

Rachel felt herself grin a chocolate bar grin.

You showed great bravery when there was danger. Without one another, we might never have escaped from the tomb. I owe you my thanks and my friendship. Father says we may come to the states next year. I hope to see you then. Ma'salaama (good-bye).
                                            Your 'sister,'
                                            Kasha

Rachel sat in Arlene's peaceful office, nibbling the candy bar in the glow of the computer screen. She clicked the 'reply' button and took a moment to gather

her thoughts. Then she typed her message on the keyboard.

Dear Kasha,

Question: Where do mummies keep their money?
Answer: In the 'Bank of the Nile.' Get it?

Now . . . about those candy bars . . .

THE END

The

TRUTH of the **QUEST**

This story is entirely fictional. The richly ornamented robe of Joseph has not been found. But the Bible states that Joseph's brothers dipped his robe in goat's blood and told their father, Jacob, that his favorite son had been attacked by a wild animal. Years later Joseph and his family were reunited in Egypt where Joseph had become a powerful ruler. He died and was buried there until his bones were returned to his father's land in modern-day Israel. You can read more about Joseph and ancient Egypt in these books:

Egyptian Tombs. Jeanne Benedict. New York: Franklin Watts, 1989, 64 pages.

Ancient Egypt, the Land and its Legacy. TGH James. Austin, Texas: University of Texas Press, 1988, 223 pages.

The Search for Ancient Egypt. Jean Vercoutter. New York: Harry N. Abrams, 1992, 207 pages.

Egypt: Land of the Pharoahs. Alexandria, Virginia: Time Life Books, 1992, 168 pages.

Pharoahs and Kings: A Biblical Quest. David M. Rohl. New York: Crown Publishers, 1995, 425 pages.